TO: BRETT AND ALLEN

*...reading
and follow
your
dreams!*

Billy's Victory

*12-25-07
To our Bret
with a bunch
of love, hugs &
kisses. Love you plenty
Mema & Pepa*

Dan Price

*Dan Price
12-8-07*

Billy's Victory

Published by Wheatmark™
610 East Delano Street, Suite 104, Tucson, Arizona 85705 U.S.A.
(888) 934-0888 ext. 3
www.wheatmark.com

ISBN: 978-1-58736-902-5
LCCN: 2007931428

Cover art by TM Creations
Interior design by Lori Sellstrom

Chapter 1

Journey to Johnsonville

Billy Ray Reynolds sat on the edge of the bank with his knees pulled up under his chin.

He spotted a dozen quail explode from the high grass at the east end of the pond. The birds flew away in search of a safer haven. They had heard the sudden sound and were quick to react.

The young boy remained in a trance for a split second longer, and then he also heard the voice from beyond the meadow.

The sound of the voice startled him, but Billy welcomed the familiar sound. It brought him back to reality.

Being in a daze was nothing new to Billy. Sometimes he found himself caught in a time machine. It was like the film in a projector…rewinding…rewinding.

He would see fragments of his young past weave in and out of his thoughts.

His mind was cluttered. Too cluttered for an 11-year-old boy.

"Come on Billy, it's time to go!"

It was his mother's voice. He loved her voice. It was soft at times...stern at times, but it was a voice that made him feel safe.

He needed her more than ever before.

Dad was gone and Billy couldn't openly explain his feelings. The words just wouldn't flow freely. Instead, he was left with a big lump in his throat as if the words were stuck behind a closed door with no way out.

It seemed like it was just the other day his mother had accused him of talking too much.

But it wasn't just the other day, it was two months ago — the last Sunday in February to be exact.

Billy remembers sitting next to his dad in the den. Chipper, the family collie, was sprawled out in front of the fireplace. His mother was busy in the kitchen making pancakes for breakfast.

It was a cold morning and the frost was just beginning to soften on the windows, allowing icy trails to make their way down into the window sills.

The wood in the fireplace was crackling and the aroma of fresh bacon had finally made its way through the hallway and into the den.

Billy's mother came out of the kitchen and walked over to her two "boys". She put her hand on her son's shoulder and said jokingly: "You're a regular little chatterbox this morning. Give your dad a break, let him finish the sports page."

John Reynolds just smiled. He was used to sharing the sports page with his son.

In fact, John had taught his son how to read a box score from top to bottom. He taught him how to figure batting averages and how to use basic math skills to calculate a pitcher's earned run average.

Billy had no problem keeping up with the statistics of his favorite baseball players. His father had seen to that.

A moment later, the phone rang and Billy watched his mother untie her apron and rush back into the kitchen to answer it.

Joan Reynolds was so excited she could hardly contain herself and call John to the phone. "John, I think it's someone from the Yankee organization," she said, proudly.

John Reynolds put down the paper, ruffled his hand over Billy's head and walked down the hallway and into the kitchen to answer the call.

After five minutes of "yes sir" and "no sir", John hung up the phone and opened up his arms to his wife and Billy. Even Chipper tried to get into the act as he stood up on all fours, barked a couple of times and wagged his tail.

The Reynolds family's dream of John making it to the major leagues was close to becoming a reality.

"Billy, the Yankees want me in St. Petersburg in two weeks for spring training," John said, grinning from ear to ear.

Billy heard his mother's voice once again. And then he heard the rattling of the old cowbell, coming from the back porch of the main house. For years, that sound meant dinner was ready. This time it meant something else.

Billy took one last look at the pond. It had been a special

place for him and his dad. Billy had caught his first fish at Oak Hollow, barely a hop, skip and a jump from the main house.

Sometimes, Billy and his dad would sit quietly on the shore and watch the Texas sun disappear below the far horizon, other times, they would use a couple of old bamboo poles, sit, and wait for a bobble, and just maybe, they'd latch on to a catfish or a nice perch for dinner.

It was time to go. His mother was calling him.

Billy began the short trek back to the house. The winding path took him through a field of marigolds and on to the north side of the barn and then it was just a quick jog around the barn and up to the main house.

His mother was waiting patiently.

"The station wagon is packed. We have to hurry or we'll miss the train," she said.

She knew her son was hurting.

Billy hadn't spoken a word since the funeral. The family doctor had said, "It will take time, just be patient…there's nothing physically wrong with your son. Give him some time, he'll sort things out."

And now, it would be tough for Billy to finally leave the ranch, the Reynolds' home for the past five years.

Joan Reynolds gave Billy a soft slap on his backside as the young boy dove into the back seat of the station wagon. Chipper followed, and Joan closed the rear doors of the vehicle.

She looked back at the ranch house, the barn, the field, and the trees that surrounded the southern edge of Oak Hollow.

Everlasting memories.

It had taken a lot of hard work and all their savings—including John's bonus—to buy the place, but they worked it out and they had their ranch house and the two-hundred and fifty acres that went with it.

It had all been worth it, until that fateful night.

Joan opened the driver's side of the station wagon. She watched a sudden gust of wind force a stubborn bush to bounce along the side of the house.

The tumbleweed seemed to pick up steam as it rolled on out past the corral and finally came to a halt at the base of the backstop next to *Billy's Field*.

It was then that Joan noticed the backstop and the black and white sign that was twirling in the wind. The sign had lost one of its two hooks and the constant breeze had forced the sign to turn over and over—banging against the very top of the backstop.

She knew she must rescue the sign. "Wait a minute, Billy. I'll be right back."

She ran over, unhooked the sign and rushed back to the station wagon.

Billy's mother put her right hand on her forehead and cleared away a strand of her blond hair from her eyes. She closed the car door and started up the engine.

She handed Billy the sign and took a deep breath: "Buckle up Billy, we're off to Grandma's."

Joan looked through the rearview mirror and watched her son rub his hands over the sign. She knew her son would find a special place for it.

She smiled as she eyed Billy's hat. The hat, with the famous Yankee emblem stenciled on the front, was turned to its side and the locks of Billy's black wavy hair extended out from under it.

She thought her son was the spitting image of John. They were alike in so many ways. Except for their height, of course. Joan remembered her husband's recent comment: "Just wait, Joan, he'll sprout up. I picked up a foot-and-a-half in junior high school alone."

She recalled John was six-feet-four and weighed 240 pounds in college. His college chums nicknamed him "Big John". She shook her head and tried to picture how Billy would look in ten years.

Manny Hernandez waited patiently at the gate. He could see the dust swirling behind the rear tires of the Reynolds' Country Squire station wagon as the vehicle grew larger and larger as it approached the north entrance to the ranch.

Manny had been the ranch foreman and all-around care-taker while John was on the road traveling from one minor league ballpark to another.

His work load was at its heaviest during the spring and summer months, but during the winter months, Manny was able to spend the majority of his time at home with his family in Rancho Cordova, a small community 10 miles south of the Reynolds' ranch.

But this day would be a sad day for Manny. With hammer and nails in hand, his final chore for the Reynolds' family would be to nail a sold sign on the gate.

Manny was short in stature, but his heart was as big as a

Texas T-bone. Billy enjoyed Manny's company and the aging Hispanic cowboy enjoyed being around Billy as well.

It was Manny who taught Billy how to rope a calf, how to ride the horses, and basically, how to take care of all the ranch animals.

Billy waved to his friend as the vehicle rolled through the gate in a cloud of dust. He wanted to tell Manny goodbye, but the words remained caught in his throat and deep in his young heart.

Instead, he continued to wave as the station wagon rolled on—the muscular figure becoming smaller, and smaller, as the dust settled over the road, blocking out the gate, the ranch, and Manny.

Billy looked down at the muddied sign and started to clean it off with a handkerchief he had found in his left coat pocket.

He thought back. It was two summers ago and his dad had been home—nursing a knee injury that would eventually keep him out of fifty games that season.

His dad worked on the field day after day for a month. With the help of the ranch hands and Manny, they transformed the pasture into a miniature ball field and put up a curved-shaped wired fence behind home plate.

And, when the job was done, his dad lifted him up and had him hook the sign into the webbing of the backstop.

"It's official," his dad said. "We'll call it Billy's Field."

During that same summer, Billy remembered his dad introducing him to "Iron Mike".

Iron Mike had been a work-in-progress for close to a year.

John had used his engineering skills picked up during his college days to put together an electronic pitching machine.

Somehow his dad, using two car tires and some kind of a motor, had rigged up a machine that would allow baseballs to spin out between the rotating tires and sail towards the plate.

Billy recalled the balls weren't always strikes. He had to do a lot of ducking now and then, but surprisingly, more times than not, the balls would fly across the plate at a high rate of speed.

Billy looked out the window of the station wagon. They were pulling into the train station. Soon, they would be leaving Texas and they would be on their way to his mother's hometown—a town called Johnsonville.

The clown had been through the ritual millions and millions of times...

It always took George Thomas much longer to put on the costumes, the shoes, and all the makeup, but when the performances were over it didn't take him very long to change from "Roscoe the Baseball Clown" back to a face more recognizable to his family and friends.

However; tonight was different.

Roscoe had just given his final performance. For thirty-five years, he had ignited the emotions of small crowds at minor league baseball parks all over the country.

Now it was time to give it up. It was time to put the clown suit back into the old green foot locker and head back to his hometown: Back to Johnsonville.

He had thrilled youngsters all over the country with his

antics. He had made thousands of strangers laugh. He knew exactly what needed to be done to jump-start a crowd and get them into the game—the game he loved: baseball.

The clown used his special oil to clear the makeup from his aging face. He had started out in his early 30s, traveling with a small-time circus, moving from town to town.

It seemed so long ago. It was at a time when his young body could tackle anything. No matter what the routine, he could handle it all gracefully, without any aches or pains.

But now, as he glanced into the makeshift mirror that hung on the wall of the visitors' locker room, the wrinkles were now signaling otherwise.

He thought back to those lonely days on the road, sitting in a cab of a truck as the convoy rolled down the highway enroute to another town, another circus...another performance.

As he rubbed a spot of soap off his forehead, the clown thought back to the early days. It was Jack Vincent, the owner of a double-A franchise in Toledo, who had helped launch Roscoe's career.

Vincent was having trouble filling up his ballpark. He tried everything from dancing girls to shooting some poor man out of a cannon. Nothing seemed to work, until Vincent got the idea to bring "Roscoe" to the park.

Not only did the idea work for Vincent as his attendance soared; but it also turned out to be the best thing for George Thomas.

The one phone call from Vincent marked the beginning of a career for "Roscoe" that would last for thirty years.

And, more importantly, it allowed George to combine "clowning around" with baseball, his number-one passion.

But, it was over now. His family needed him. Billy needed him. It was the end of April. It was the beginning of the season for the Stockton Bison, and a new clown had been hired to replace George.

George had heard the new "mascot" would be wearing antlers and he was supposed to roam around the stadium and "snort" at the fans.

George wished he could stick around for a week just to see the new clown in action.

"George, the taxi is here," said Jimmy Slater, a jack-of-all-trades around Stockton Stadium. "I'll be back in a minute to give you a hand with that old trunk of yours."

George was glad for the help, but he also knew Jimmy had his hands full closing down the park. The Stockton Bison had just won the game, 6-3, over the visiting Edmonton Trackers and George, as usual, had thrilled 3,000 fans during the pre-game festivities.

But this time, George would definitely wait for Jimmy's help. The trunk was full to the gills and it was a long walk up the stairs, out the turnstiles and on to the street where the cab was waiting.

Jimmy Slater had found two stadium workers to help haul George's belongings curbside, much to the delight of the cab driver, who had been waiting patiently for his next customer.

"We will miss you," said Slater. "You were certainly a fixture around here and I'm pretty sure there are many, many more owners of these old ballparks around the country that would say the same."

George thought it was nice to hear those kind words. That, of course, had been George's intention all along. After all, that's what clowns are supposed to do—leave a lasting impression.

With Jimmy at his side, George stopped and peeked through the walkway one more time. George's eyes focused on the beautiful, well-manicured infield, surrounded by the plush green carpet-like outfield.

George had always thought there was a slight resemblance between Stockton Stadium and Chicago's Wrigley Field. Well, in a miniature sort of way, that is.

Maybe it was those old rafters, or maybe, it was just those old-time bleachers behind home plate. There was something about the old ballpark that made him think of Wrigley.

But, then again, after one look at the sign in center field, it wouldn't take George long to discount those thoughts. Painted across the sign were the words: Eat at Joe's Bar and Grill.

George shook hands with Jimmy for the final time and climbed into the cab. "Airport please, I'm going home."

George settled into his window seat on the twin-engine Convair 580. The fifty-passenger propeller aircraft was one of his favorite rides. Leave those new fangled fast-moving jets to the "jet-setters". The old clown was quite content with the lower-to-the-ground flying machines.

It would be a while before the plane would reach southern Colorado and eventually land at the little regional airport, just a few miles north of Johnsonville.

George would have plenty of time to get some shut-eye. It had been a long, emotional day and the weeks ahead would be more of the same.

The old clown placed the pillow next to the window. He found a comfortable position and fell fast asleep.

Within minutes, the reoccurring dream materialized...

Smoke, or was it just clouds swirling? The dream would always start out the same. In the distance was a huge figure moving forward, ever so slowly. Where was the figure coming from and, more importantly, where was it going? Close by, another figure would appear, smaller in stature, but just as intriguing. And the voices, not just one or two, but a group, cheering in unison.

"Sir, would you like some coffee?

George awoke. It was the redheaded stewardess, the one that had so kindly offered him the pillow moments ago. Or, was it hours ago?

"We will be landing in Johnsonville about an hour from now," she said.

Billy loved riding on trains. He could count on one hand how many passenger trains he had been on. This would be number five. He had been on two train rides to watch his dad play ball and there were two other times when he went on tour with his famous Grandpa Thomas.

The trips were always exciting.

But this time, Billy sat quietly. He laid his head back and focused his eyes out the window and watched the land disappear behind him as the locomotive rolled toward its destination.

He felt a warm hand on his cheek as his mother reached over and lovingly said, "We'll be home soon."

Billy eyes closed. It wasn't long before the dream would appear...

A field, green in color—covered in a cloudy mist—could be seen in the distance. A small figure tried desperately to maneuver up a flight of steps, but continued to slip and fall back into a dark hole. Finally, after many attempts, the figure was successful. The figure reached the top of the steps, regained its footing, and raced toward the open field. Standing at the far end of the field was another figure. Tall, dark and mysterious, the figure was on the move, taking slow and deliberate steps toward the center of the field.

The smaller figured continued to run hard and fast, but it never seemed to gain any ground. The dark figure remained far away. The clouds returned, canvassing the field, and the small figure would come to a halt, turn, and return to the base of the steps and vanish back into the black hole.

Billy's body began to quiver.

"Wake up...wake up, Billy, you're having that dream again," his mother said with a concerned look.

Billy opened his eyes. He was back on the train, back in seat 4A—steamrolling toward Johnsonville.

Johnsonville was a quiet, pleasant town, located at the base of a mountain range near the Colorado-Utah border.

The town's residents enjoyed all the seasons—fall, winter, spring and especially summer, for the summer meant balmy weather, plenty of sunshine, and, of course...baseball.

The athletes at Johnsonville High School did the best they could during the year to give the locals something to cheer about, but more times than not, they were forced to play the "underdog" role and usually found themselves on the short end of the stick.

Due to the size of the enrollment, the school couldn't field a football team and the coaches spent a lot of their time recruiting in the hallways in hopes of coming up with a big enough roster to compete against the nearby schools in basketball and baseball.

So, when it came to sports, the Johnsonville residents really didn't have a lot to cheer about on a daily basis. But little did they know, a new resident would be stepping off the train in a few hours that would turn the summer into a summer to remember.

It was only eight o'clock Monday morning and barber Ted Carrillo already had them three deep and was completing the final touches on what little hair Johnsonville bank president Jonathan Holmes had left, when the conversation came up regarding the town's anticipated population explosion.

"Jonathan, did you hear Joan Reynolds and her son, Billy, are coming to town?" Ted said. "They'll be in on the noon train and George is flying in from California to be with them. He's hanging up that clown suit for good."

The three gentlemen, who were waiting for their turn in the barber chair, had spent the last three days helping Claire Thomas prepare for the arrival of her daughter and grandson as well as her husband's return. The three men were well aware of the recent events that had turned the lives of the town's most famous family upside down.

After all, Claire Thomas was the town's leading lady, so to speak. She owned the only drugstore in the community and was currently in her fourth term as the vice-mayor.

The local townsfolk were simply amazed at the woman's energy level. She was always on the go. She kept Mayor Ezra Lockhart on his toes, kept three full-time employees in check at the drugstore and kept her home in perfect order while her husband was away.

The three gentlemen, fire chief Johnny Hayes; hardware and clothing store owner Cyrus Jones; and Little League coach Carl Perkins, were all former grade school and high school classmates of Claire and George Thomas.

With more than fifty years of friendship in the books, there was no question that everyone in the barbershop, and in town as well, would be going out of their way to make the family's homecoming as comfortable as possible.

The train rolled on…

Joan Reynolds noticed that Billy had fallen back to sleep. She hoped he would sleep comfortably the remainder of the trip. As for her, there would be no sleep. She leaned her head back, took a deep breath, and suddenly, that fateful night was upon her.

The highway patrol officer took off his hat and ran his right hand over the brim of his Stetson in hopes of gaining an extra moment before bellowing out the words, "Mrs. Reynolds, there's been an accident."

On a rain-drenched stretch of highway, just east of the

Texas-Arkansas border, the driver of a semi truck had lost control and crossed the centerline. The driver of the eastbound car was John Reynolds.

John was gone.

Up until that moment, Joan's life had been picture-perfect. A small town girl, Joan was raised in the happiest of homes. Her father, full of wit and charm, was born with a special gift. He could make everyone laugh.

Joan recalls, when the subject of her father would come up, she would always say, "If you can't laugh around my dad, you're not human."

Her mother, on the other hand, was the taskmaster of the family. There was nothing she couldn't handle. The ability to press on was her major strength and Joan was counting on that family trait to carry her through the tough times ahead.

Joan knew she'd led a storybook life. She graduated at the top of her class in high school, went to college and fell in love with the star of the baseball team.

John and Joan were married in a beautiful ceremony in San Diego, California, followed by a week-long honeymoon in Hawaii.

Joan recalls two days after the honeymoon, her husband began a 10-day road trip and a start to a 110-game schedule with a Class-A team out of Visalia, California.

A year later, Billy Ray was born. It was the happiest day of the young couple's life.

Joan remembered how hard it was for John to be away from the family. During those early years on the road, he constantly relied on late-night phone calls to keep abreast of what was happening on the home front.

But the adjustments were made and the young family worked it out. After all, baseball was becoming their livelihood.

After a couple of seasons, John was making a few heads turn and was soon promoted to Double-A. It wasn't long before John and Joan made the offer on the ranch and headed for Texas.

Then trouble struck. Shoulder injuries. Knee injuries. Rehabilitation...followed by more injuries. Then came all the whispering from the "movers and shakers" in the Yankee organization. "He might be through. His arm is gone. He won't be able to run on that knee."

But Joan recalled how strong John was, mentally as well as physically. Even during the worst of times, he would fight through it all, press on and push himself toward that dream of his—to play ball in the majors and play for the Yankees.

He was so determined. Twelve years in the minors—five of those years saddled with career-threatening injuries before he finally got the call he was waiting for.

Big John Reynolds would have been a 32-year-old rookie.

Billy's mother felt someone brush by her. It was the train conductor enroute to the next car. She realized she had been deep in thought. She rubbed both her eyes, and massaged the back of her neck.

Joan looked up and down the aisle of the passenger compartment. The seats were full of people heading for one destination or another—all of them with hopes and dreams and lives of their own to fulfill.

Joan, of course, had her destination all mapped out. She knew where she was going, and she knew, sitting alongside her was a very special passenger. She was heading to a place that would surround her and Billy with a loving family and many, many friends.

She hoped, in time, that Billy would win his battle within himself, and in turn, would take on new dreams, set new goals for himself and look forward to the future.

Joan couldn't think of a better place than Johnsonville to return Billy to reality. Johnsonville was where it all began for her. Would Billy's new surroundings provide the right ingredients to bring the young boy back?

Joan was counting on it.

Chapter 2

The Homecoming

Claire looked at her watch as she pulled the Crown Victoria sedan into her usual parking spot. The parking stall was not marked, but everyone in town recognized her car, and the local residents were kind enough to park their vehicles elsewhere.

From time to time, an unsuspecting out-of-towner would slip into the spot, but Claire would pay them no mind. After all, this was Johnsonville, not New York City.

Still, it was Claire's favorite spot; a few quick steps and she'd be at the front door of her drugstore.

Claire couldn't believe the time. It was nine o'clock.

Luckily, teenager Timmy Watson was scheduled to open the store. She once again would be blessed with great summer help. Timmy had just a few afternoon classes left at school. It was the final week of school and he had his mornings free to make a little extra spending money.

21

Of course, during the winter, fall and early spring, George was always home to help her run the business.

Claire got out of her car. As she scurried to the entrance of the drugstore, she noticed how quiet Main Street was for a Monday morning.

Claire looked across the street and could see a few heads bobbing up and down in the barbershop. The Johnsonville Café, just four doors down from the drugstore, had a few patrons, but all in all—a nice quiet morning.

Claire said good morning to Timmy and headed directly for her office, located in the back of the store.

She didn't have a lot of time to spare. She had to pick up George at the airport in about an hour and a half, and Joan and Billy would be pulling into the train station around noon.

Claire finished up the cash deposit from the weekend, wrote out a note for her pharmacist, Oren Crane, who would be in at ten o'clock, gave Timmy a hug, and rushed out the front door. The chimes on the top of the door rattled, signaling her hasty departure.

"It's your turn, Carl," the barber said, as Mr. Perkins put down the morning paper and moved ever so gently into Ted's chair.

"You go easy on me. I want the boys to still recognize me."

Coach Perkins was one of the few old-timers in town who was still sporting a healthy head of hair and he wanted to keep it that way.

Carl was aware of the promise he'd given his current batch

of Little Leaguers at their first practice last week. He had told them: "Win the District title and I'll shave my head."

But for now, Carl ordered: "Ted, trim a little off the top and up the sideburns."

Ted shook off the apron and placed it around Carl's shoulders. The barber had taken care of Johnny Hayes and Cyrus Jones in record fashion, as both men had hustled out of the shop and off to work, allowing Ted to concentrate on his next victim.

Ted positioned the chair in such away to allow both of them a clear view of Main Street.

"Look, there goes Claire. It won't be long before the family will be together."

Carl smiled. He couldn't wait to hear what Joan and Billy had to say about their new home over on Fourth Street.

Carl, Johnny and Cyrus had spent the last three days fixing up Joan and Billy's new residence—an old Victorian-style two-bedroom house, recently purchased by the Reynolds' family.

The house was ready for its new owners.

Even the Mayflower moving van had rolled in to town on Saturday and had dropped off all the Reynolds' furniture.

Everything had worked out perfectly.

Carl looked up at Ted and beamed.

"It should be a great homecoming."

George's plane was right on schedule.

Claire waited by the gate as she watched the ladder from the aircraft open up like an accordion and fall softly to the ground.

The aircraft was full of passengers, but most of them were continuing on to another destination. Six deplaned, and George was the last passenger to find his way through the aisle and down the steps.

The old clown maneuvered his way toward the gate and met his wife with open arms.

"It's good to be home. Now, let's go help our grandson."

The train slowed. Billy glanced out the window. He could see people scurrying about as the train rolled to a stop.

Billy gripped his mother's arm with his right hand and placed his index finger of his left hand on the window.

Joan leaned over. "There's Grandma and Grandpa."

Billy's mother detected a slight smile on the face of her son. She took a deep sigh and began to gather up their belongings. Finally, when the aisle was clear, Billy and Joan raced to the front of the passenger car, down the steps and into the loving arms of George and Claire.

Billy sat quietly in the back seat of Grandma's car. Still sporting that slight grin, he listened attentively to his grandpa as the Crown Victoria rolled toward Johnsonville.

"Billy, we've got a nice surprise for you and your mom."

Billy wondered what that could be.

As for Joan, she leaned forward and took one look at her mom, and then her dad. "All right, what are you two up to?"

George turned his head and gave his daughter one of those famous "Roscoe the Clown" grins. "Patience...patience, you'll just have to wait and see."

George winked at Claire and then turned his attention back to the road. Billy looked out the window, just in time to see a highway sign whiz by. The sign read: Johnsonville, 5 miles.

Joan was home.

She put her arm around Billy as her father took the first Johnsonville exit off the interstate. George turned left onto First Street and drove past the old courthouse, the town library, and then made a right turn and headed down Lafayette Lane.

He passed the fire station, the police station, the elementary school and the high school, and finally, he weaved his way over Rainbow Bridge and into Johnson Park.

George wanted Billy to see the park. It was Johnsonville's pride and joy.

Constructed a decade ago, the park had beautiful, tall oak trees at one end with plenty of bicycle paths and running trails for the local Johnsonville residents to take advantage of.

At the other end was the baseball field, complete with freshly painted bleachers that went all the way up and down the first and third base lines.

The field was in immaculate condition. The infield was covered in brown clay and the outfield's emerald green grass had recently been cut.

George slowed down the car and he looked back at Billy. Billy was sitting on his hands and knees, his eyes focused, staring directly at the ball field.

The old clown knew what he was doing. So did Claire

and Joan. Billy remained silent, but his insides were churning. George's little tour through town had made an impression on Billy. And, it was just the beginning…

George took the south exit out of the park. He drove down Orchard Lane and sped past Johnsonville's new minimall, which included a new grocery store, a pizza parlor, an ice cream shop and a movie theater.

He turned right on Loretta Drive and then left onto Fourth Street. At the end of the cul-de-sac was Billy's new home, nestled behind two giant oak trees.

George pulled into the driveway.

"Well, what do you think?"

Joan put both her hands over her face. She was elated. "Mom and dad, you did good."

Joan had known all along about the house. She just hadn't seen it with her own eyes. John's business partner, Robert Lipton, had quickly stepped in—just days after the funeral, and assured Joan that her business affairs would be taken care of.

Lipton, in record time, finalized the sale of the ranch, and, with the additional help of George and Claire, was able to complete both transactions, just a week before Joan and Billy were scheduled to leave for Johnsonville.

As for Billy, it was all a complete surprise. Billy walked alongside the grownups as they all ventured up the sidewalk and onto the red-colored porch. At the end of the porch, Billy saw a white-painted swing; it hung from the rafters and looked strong enough to handle two people, maybe three.

The family reached the front door and Grandpa Thomas handed Joan the keys and said, "Be my guest."

The entry way opened up into a huge living room area. Billy noticed the furniture—the leather couch, the rocking chair, the end tables, everything was in its place.

A small dining area was off to the left. Mom's favorite china cabinet was there along with the maple table and six chairs.

The kitchen was at the far end of the house. The tall refrigerator was there. Billy would always need a foot stool to reach the ice cream bars. The foot stool was wedged in the corner, next to the sink.

Billy ran to the back of the house and found a huge sitting-room with a fireplace. The television was there, and on one of the end tables, Billy noticed the new fangled remote control gadget that had come with the RCA television his dad had purchased last year.

Billy moved quickly and within a few seconds had surveyed the entire first floor.

He checked out the big backyard, which was surrounded by a three-foot high white picket fence. In the corner of the yard was a doghouse, big enough for Chipper to wiggle into.

"It looks like this will be a great place for Chipper, too," Joan said to Billy, as she watched her son re-enter the house from the screened-in back porch.

If there was one cog in the day's extraordinary events, it was the fact that the train conductor had advised Joan that Chipper would be arriving late, thanks to a cargo mix-up.

Joan had assured Billy that Chipper would arrive on tomorrow's train. Seeing Chipper's new doghouse had made Billy feel a lot better about that situation.

Grandpa Thomas put his hand on Billy's shoulder. "Are you ready to see your room?"

George, Claire and Joan were all smiles as they followed Billy up the giant staircase.

Billy counted each step, twenty-five in all, he added, as he made his way to the top.

To the left, he could see his mother's new bedroom. In the center of the hallway, a nice big bathroom, containing an oval-shaped bath tub, big enough, Billy thought, to give Chipper a bath in.

At the opposite end of the hallway was Billy's room. With Billy leading the way, the family entered the room.

Billy stopped in his tracks. Joan put her right arm around her mother. "Mom, this is your handy-work, isn't it?"

"I had plenty of help, but it was surely a race against time once the moving van arrived. But, I must say," as tears trickled down her cheek, "it was all worth it."

Claire nudged Billy. "You go on in and check your room out. You'll see, it is not much different than your room back in Texas."

Billy walked slowly over to his bed and sat down.

"I wasn't sure where to put all those baseball cards," his grandma said. "But there are plenty of secret, little hiding places around. You'll just have to snoop around a little."

Billy waited for the grownups to head downstairs before he started to explore his new domicile.

"I'll put the coffee pot on," George said. "You two sit down and take a load off."

Claire and Joan had no trouble granting that request as

they pulled a couple of chairs out and sat down at the kitchen table.

Claire chuckled as she heard noise coming from Billy's room. "You know, Joan, we had a lot of help getting this place in shape. Johnny, Cyrus and Carl painted the walls, scrubbed the floors, unpacked tons of boxes, you name it, and they did it. They're an amazing trio.

"But, I must warn you. The garage is a mess. It'll take a month of Sundays to get that place in order. About the only thing you can get your hands on is Billy's bike, and I have a feeling he's going to want that right away."

Joan shook her head. She just couldn't believe her parent's life-long friends, Johnny, Cyrus and Carl. They were always willing to go the extra mile to help out. Joan had a name for the trio, she called them "The Three Musketeers."

"I think the garage can wait," Joan said. "Manny promised to bring the station wagon to us in a couple of weeks. He made arrangements to drop it off, and he's scheduled a flight out of here, so he can visit his sister over in Modesto. That'll give us plenty of time to work on the garage."

Claire looked over at her tiring husband. "Well, honey, I think we've done all the damage we can do here. I think we need to get you home to bed. We'll have to wait until tomorrow to get you unpacked. Billy will probably be over the first thing in the morning to help you unpack that footlocker."

Joan kissed her parents goodbye and waved to them as they pulled out of the driveway and headed home.

They didn't have far to go. Billy would soon find that out. Up Loretta Drive, right on Auburn Hills Road and then a quick five minutes up the hill in third gear on his bike would put him at his grandparent's front doorstep.

Joan could still hear Billy scurrying around upstairs, so she poured herself another cup of coffee and sat back down at the kitchen table.

She would need to fix dinner soon. Her mom had been so kind to even fill the refrigerator with food. They had lunch on the train, but that was hours ago.

She looked out the kitchen window. The sun was setting and a flock of geese flew across the now shadowy sky.

Such a peaceful place, she thought. It was great to be home. It was great to see her folks again. They had been together at the funeral just two months ago. They had all said their goodbyes to John…together.

Now it was time to begin again for Billy's sake. Today had been a very good start.

Billy felt at ease in his new surroundings. Grandma Thomas had seen to that. Billy looked around at his new room.

Billy's life-sized vintage posters—one of his dad hitting a homerun during a game against Evansville three years ago and the other of Mickey Mantle and Roger Maris, taken at Yankee Stadium last year—were carefully placed on the wall next to his bed.

His grandmother had centered his wooden dresser under the window. Billy looked out the window. He had a perfect view of the backyard. Just outside the back gate was a steep hill. Beyond the hill, stood the forest—populated with hundreds of tall trees, which covered the far horizon and blocked out the late-afternoon sunlight.

Billy checked out the baseballs, which were sitting proudly on stands on the top of his dresser. Billy took a rag from the top drawer and made sure each trophy was spotless—each autographed ball marking an important milestone in his dad's baseball career.

Each ball dated and placed in chronological order from left to right.

On the wall, across from his bed, were framed pictures—some were of his dad playing ball; some were of his grandpa performing in one of his many clown outfits—all placed neatly in a row, one after another.

Billy then proceeded to check out all his dresser drawers. His shirts, socks and underwear were all there. And his glove, where was it? He frantically searched. Second drawer, no. Third drawer, no. Fourth drawer, yes. There it was, in the left hand corner, tucked away under his flannel pajamas.

He remembered he had sat in the den—back at the ranch—next to his dad, oiling the glove the night before his dad was to leave for spring training in Florida.

The glove was a Rawlings with a soft pocket. It fit his hand perfectly. He took a deep breath and placed the glove back in its rightful place.

Billy looked around the room. Everything was in its place. But what should he do with his prize collection of baseball cards?

His dad had told him many times. "You got a fine collection of cards, you hold on to those. Those cards will be worth some money someday."

At the ranch, he had a special hiding place. But here, where should he put them?

He checked the closet. Grandma Claire had put all his clothes on hangers, and his shoes were also neatly placed at one end of the closet.

And then he saw it. At the other end of the closet one of the wooden slats was loose. His grandma had said, "to snoop". So, snoop he did.

Billy pulled up the board...and then another...and then another. He looked down into the opening. He figured the space to be about three feet long and about ten inches deep. It was plenty of room for the cards and then some.

He quickly got up, brought the boxes of cards from on top his bed and began to put them into his new hiding place.

He pushed the boards back into place. Mission accomplished.

He could smell the aroma of his mother's cooking. It was time to eat. Billy surveyed the room one more time, closed the door and headed downstairs.

"It sounded like you were a busy little beaver up there," Joan said, as she placed a sizzling hamburger and fries in front of his nose.

She should've come up with a more balanced meal, but it was Billy's favorite and his first night in his new home...so she gave in.

She knew Billy would eat a hamburger and fries for breakfast if he could get away with it.

Billy's father had always seen to it that his son understood the reasoning behind good eating habits. Joan's husband was the stronger of the two of them when it came to that.

"Vegetables, and more vegetables, that'll make you a stronger hitter, and carrots will help you improve your eyesight and allow you to pick up the pitch."

Joan knew Billy listened to every word. And most of the time, Billy would adhere to his dad's requests to finish all the food on his plate.

But one thing was for sure: Billy loved hamburgers.

Joan watched her son finish off the burger. She smiled and said: "Now go up and try out the tub. I put some fresh towels on the sink for you."

By nine o'clock, Billy was ready for bed. His mom walked in the room, and instantly she realized Billy had gone over his room with a fine-tooth comb—everything was put away, all nice and tidy.

He had found his radio and placed it on his nightstand, next to the lamp. On the other nightstand sat a photograph. The photo was of his father, looking strong and confident, holding a Louisville Slugger over his right shoulder. Next to the photo was the *Billy's Field* sign, cleaned and polished— and not a mark on it.

Joan was amazed how Billy continued to go out of his way to keep his things—and his dad's things—in order.

She knew of only one person who would go to those extremes—her father.

Joan gave Billy a kiss, turned off the light and closed the door.

Billy put his head on the pillow, pulled up the covers and

quickly went to sleep. The dream returned. But this time there was no black hole...

The figure stood very still in the open field. It seemed to be staring upwards toward the heavens. White, fluffy clouds rolled by, leaving behind a beautiful blue sky. The figure was wearing a pinstripe uniform with a number 8 stenciled on its back. The figure looked back. The steps were gone. The black hole was gone. The figure saw nothing, except for a low-lying mist that moved slowly across the field. The figure could hear a crowd cheering in the distance...

Billy opened his eyes for a moment. He glanced over at the photo of his father. He closed his eyes and fell back to sleep.

Chapter 3

The Clown's Den

Billy was up early the next morning. He ate break-fast with his mom. He helped her with the dishes, grabbed his baseball hat and headed for the garage.

He found his bicycle easily enough. It was lying on its side next to a couple of huge boxes, but luckily, he was able to push them aside and free his bike.

Billy began his first full day in Johnsonville helping his grandpa unpack the old green locker.

It had taken Billy only five minutes to cruise over to his grandparent's house, which was situated on top of a hill, surrounded by an acre of densely-populated trees.

Behind the main house was a rectangular building. Four large railroad ties embedded in the ground led to the porch.

Billy's mother had warned him, "Grandma Thomas may not be home. Your grandma will probably be at the drugstore, but chances are your grandpa will be around back in that old building of his."

Sure enough, that's where Billy found him. Billy gently turned his bike on its side and ventured up the steps.

Billy reached the porch and looked up at a yellow sign that was nailed to the door. Written on the sign were three words: *The Clown's Den*.

Billy opened the door and his eyes popped wide open.

The inside of the building was a lot bigger than Billy had expected. It wasn't just one room, but four separate rooms. All the rooms had wood floors. The floors let off a shiny glow. They had recently been waxed.

Pinned to the walls in the first room were hundreds of clown costumes. The costumes were in all sizes, shapes, and colors.

Billy moved to the second room. The room was full of autographed photos of clowns, all of them showing off and smiling from ear to ear.

It was a clown's hall of fame.

But that wasn't all.

Billy moved to the third room. The wall to the left contained photographs of professional baseball players, each picture autographed and signed: to George, with love.

Billy looked to the right and saw an assortment of glass cases—each of them containing tools of the trade, from catcher's mitts, to first baseman's gloves, to bats, to balls, and even a base or two, including a pitching rubber and a home plate.

Billy gingerly moved into the fourth room. Grandpa

Thomas was sitting in a rocking chair in front of an old leather desk, wiping the perspiration off his brow.

"There you are, I've almost got this locker unloaded. I hope you had a good night's sleep. I'm going to keep you pretty busy today. There's a lot to see and do."

Billy looked around the room. It looked more like an office compared to the other three rooms.

The shelf on the right side of the room housed a Philco radio, much like the one he had on his nightstand in his bedroom. He wondered if his grandpa could tune in games like he did.

Billy recalled that sometimes he would spend hours trying to break through the radio's static in hopes of picking up a ball game.

It didn't matter—a college game, a minor league game, a major league game—wherever he could find a baseball game, he'd tune it in and listen.

George caught Billy eyeing the old Philco.

"Billy, that radio has been good to me over the years. I've picked up a lot of games with that old Philco. I'm sure we'll be giving it a try this summer. With that mountain range behind us, sometimes it's tough to pick anything up."

Billy continued to look around the room as his grandpa got up and put both his hands on the shoulders of the young man.

Next to the radio were framed pictures of a little boy. "Those are all of you, Billy."

And on the far wall, behind the desk, Billy eyed a family portrait. The photo included grandpa, his father, mother and Grandma Claire.

Billy remembered when the photo was taken. "Stop squirming, sit still," his mother had said. It was taken last Christmas, just four months ago.

"That's my favorite picture," George said, as he watched Billy wander over to the portrait.

Billy stopped and looked up at the family portrait. He put his right hand on the picture and proceeded to move his hand across the image, until his fingertips had reached the smiling face of his father.

George quickly wiped away the tears which had suddenly appeared. He pulled a handkerchief out of his pocket and wiped away the remaining remnants, shielding his face from Billy.

"Come on Billy, I want you to say hello to Belle."

Belle. What's Belle? Billy thought to himself.

Billy turned away from the portrait and noticed his grandpa was pointing to the back door.

Billy didn't have a clue who, or what Belle was, but he was interested and he quickly followed his grandpa out the back door and into a tent-like covered carport.

And there, on an elongated cement slab, sat Belle — a Willys' jeep.

"That's Belle...I think she's been around longer than I have," George said proudly.

"I picked her up at an auction back in my circus days, and she's been with me ever since. Belle has been in more parades than I can shake a stick at, and I know for a fact that she's logged her share of miles for the military, long before I got ahold of her."

Billy walked slowly around Belle, allowing his hands to touch the vehicle, ever so slightly.

"Go ahead, jump in."

At 4-foot-8, Billy barely had the size to maneuver his way into the driver's seat, but by bending both legs, he was able to spring up, and in. He put both hands on Belle's steering wheel.

George noticed a smile on his grandson's face—a smile big enough to allow a familiar dimple to pop out in the youngster's cheek.

George recalled a few years back when he had asked Billy, "Where's your dimples?"

Billy quickly replied, "I got em."

George couldn't wait to tell his wife and his daughter what he had just witnessed.

George hoped it wouldn't be too much longer before the entire family would get a chance to see both dimples.

"Come on, Billy, let's go back inside and unpack the rest of the trunk."

Billy had so many questions he wanted to ask his grandpa. He wanted to know about the pictures of the clowns; the colorful costumes; the men in all the baseball photos; and all those beautiful cases.

How was grandpa able to get ahold of all that stuff? He was fascinated. He wanted to know the stories behind them all.

If Billy could have gotten the words out, he would surely tell his grandpa, *"Roscoe"*, how "cool" it was to be in the *Clown's Den*.

Billy helped his grandpa clean out the rest of the trunk.

His grandpa referred to the remaining items in the locker as "props". He said it was stuff he used in his skits to make people laugh.

George gave Billy a few light chores to do around the office. Billy worked fast, because his grandpa had offered to take him for an afternoon ride in Belle.

The three would soon head for Willow Creek and yet another adventure for Billy.

George pulled Belle into a parking spot across from the drugstore. Billy jumped out of the jeep and followed his grandpa. The two of them jogged across the street toward the entrance to the store.

A sudden gust of wind moved the sign above the front door to and fro. Billy looked up at the sign, it read: *Claire's Fountain and Drug.*

Today had already been a full day, and now grandpa promised an ice cream soda and a visit with grandma before they would head off to Willow Creek.

Claire was busy cleaning glasses when Billy and George walked in. "Hey, you two, I bet you guys are on you way up to Willow Creek."

She stopped what she was doing, and started to scramble around, looking for a scoop to measure out the ice cream for the chocolate sodas.

"I see you got Belle with you. George, it looks like I'm stuck here the rest of the day, and I just got a call from the train station. Chipper arrived and he's evidently awaiting a friendly face to show up."

"That's great, we got plenty of time to pick up Chipper

and get out to Willow Creek and back," George assured Claire.

"It'll do Chipper good. I'm sure he doesn't like being stuck in that cage of his."

Billy had already downed the soda and was ready to head for the train station.

Claire gave her favorite two men a hug and booted them out the door. She quickly got on the phone, called Joan, and advised her how Billy and her dad were doing.

Billy thought Chipper looked in pretty good shape. It didn't take long to pick up Chipper, get him out of the cage and into Belle's big open space behind the seats.

And then it was off to Willow Creek.

It was about a twenty-minute drive to George's favorite hideaway. There was only one way in and one way out, as the dirt road weaved its way around the outskirts of Johnsonville, through the forest, down a steep embankment and eventually came to an end within a stone's throw of the Colorado River.

Billy could see the river clearly as he stood up in Belle's passenger seat. He could also hear the roar of the water as the river moved its way downstream.

There was a meadow separating Willow Creek from the river and a small steady stream of water dissected its way downward into a beautiful pond that looked a lot like Oak Hollow.

"I love it out here," said George as he watched Chipper high-tail it out of the jeep and head for the meadow.

"It's nice and peaceful—and the fishing is pretty good,

too. You need a good old jeep to get in here, and Belle is just the ticket—she can certainly handle that last mile of rough road."

George looked at Billy and he could tell the boy was thinking about the ranch and Oak Hollow.

George was hoping Billy had found a new place, a new Oak Hollow.

"Billy, you see those two tall trees at the end of the meadow? Well, if you look just to the right, you'll see a couple of bushes. On the other side of the bushes is a secret path that leads back to town."

Billy stood up and looked in the direction his grandpa was pointing. He could see Chipper running by the bushes and then disappearing into the tall weeds, only to quickly reappear as he continued to circle the meadow, enjoying his freedom and a life away from his cage and those scary trains.

"That path will actually take you back to the center of town. You go through the forest and come out at Nob Hill, and take the path down the hill and end up at the north end of Main Street. You'll end up just a block away from Grandma's drugstore."

George promised to bring Billy and Chipper back to Willow Creek later in the week, along with a couple of rods and reels and some fancy lures.

George knew the sun was beginning its gradual descent, and he knew they'd only have about thirty minutes of sunlight left.

The three of them piled into the jeep and headed back to town.

After Billy's first full day in Johnsonville, George figured his grandson just might be inquisitive enough to venture out on his own.

He was right.

Billy spent the next few weeks canvassing the area. He checked out all the streets in town to see where they led.

He explored the library, the courthouse, and even visited the printing room of the town's weekly paper, The Chronicle.

Billy was seen just about everywhere. He was logging plenty of miles on his bicycle. You could hear him coming, too. Attached to the wheels of his bike were a couple of old baseball cards—flapping in the breeze. Of course, the cards were duplicates of ones he already had hidden away in the closet. But still, they served a nice purpose.

Billy didn't know it, but there were plenty of people keeping a watchful eye on the town's newest resident.

Grandpa Thomas would show up with Belle on Tuesday and Thursday mornings; They would head out to Willow Creek and sit on the smooth rocks near the pond's shoreline and fish to their hearts' content.

Billy also started cycling into town, usually on Wednesday or Thursday mornings. He would pull up in front of Cyrus Jones' hardware store and wait for the "Three Musketeers".

He found out rather quickly that the trio would show up between ten and eleven o'clock every morning and sit on Cyrus's bench outside the store, and according to what his mother had told him, " 'They sit there and solve the world's problems'."

Billy wasn't sure why his mom referred to Cyrus, Johnny and Carl as the "Musketeers" until he discovered the reason—the trio had a hankering for a certain candy bar.

He thought at first that his three new buddies were somehow descendents of pirates from the High Seas, but when he discovered the candy bar wrappers in the trash can next to the bench, he was able to figure out that his mother was poking fun at her three friends.

On the weekends, Billy would ride his bike to the south entrance of Johnson Park and take the path that led to the tall oak trees.

He would find a tree with the biggest trunk and hide behind it. He would then peek around the huge tree to catch a glimpse of the baseball field.

Sometimes he would watch a father and son playing catch, and sometimes, in the late afternoon, he might see Carl Perkins holding baseball practice with what looked to be about ten kids. Most of the kids seemed to be a little older than him.

They were all taller. They seemed to know what they were doing as Coach Perkins methodically put the players through round after round of infield and outfield practice.

Billy watched to see if the outfielders could hit their cutoff man. His keen eyes checked on the infielders to see if they kept their glove down and followed the ball into their mitt before even thinking about making a throw.

He watched all the players to see if they backed up their teammates in case of a wild throw or an error. Making an error was one thing, Billy thought, but allowing a runner an extra base because of it, was not good baseball.

Sometimes, he would hang around the trees a little longer and watch the Little Leaguers take batting practice.

On one Saturday in particular, he hid his bike and settled in behind the nearest tree to the ball field and watched each player take their cuts.

He checked out their stance in the box. He checked to see if their elbow was up, and when they did swing, did they keep their right foot planted, or, were they bailing out?

Billy knew all these things. His father had taught him well, and yet, the young boy had never played one single inning of organized baseball.

He not only learned the game of baseball from his dad, but he also was given the opportunity to learn some of the finer points of the game from his dad's teammates, all of whom were professional players in their own right.

Billy couldn't always travel with his dad, but when he did, he made every moment count.

He sat in dugouts in many minor league ballparks across the country. He studied the infielders, the outfielders, the pitchers and the catchers.

He watched the managers manage and the coaches coach. He studied how skillfully a manager would handle a routine infield practice.

Billy thought it was a thing of beauty to watch the manager juggle the bat in one hand and the ball in the other, without dropping either one. Around the horn the ball would go—a ground ball to third, then to short, then to second and finally a bouncer to first.

The infielders were always ready. Each player would gobble up the grounder and throw home.

The manager would keep it going. This time the infielders would make their strong throws to first base.

Then, the manager would work on the double play. He'd
rip a one-hopper to third. The third-sacker would field the
ball cleanly and send a snap throw to second. The second
baseman would take the throw, pivot, and relay the ball to
first.

Next, it was the shortstop's turn to start the double play,
and then the second baseman would then get his chance.

Finally, the hardest double play of them all — the grounder to first base. The first-sacker would scoop up the ball,
turn, and throw to second. The shortstop would cover, step
on the bag and throw the ball back to first into the glove of
the second baseman, whose job was to hustle over to first to
cover the bag and complete the play.

Practice and more practice...

That's what all the professional managers, players and
coaches told Billy. "If you practice enough that glove of
yours will seem like an extension of your arm," said one of
his dad's managers, during a three-game series in Shreve-
port last year.

Billy put everything he was told into the back of his mind;
he stored it all away — he had his own baseball library.

One thing his dad had told him was to strive to be the
complete player — run, hit, throw and field.

Billy's dad had always said to him: "The pros are looking
for the total package."

And as the players beyond the oak trees continued taking their cuts, Billy remembered back to "Iron Mike" and

how his dad filled the machine with a bucket of balls at Billy's Field.

Billy stepped into the box and awaited every pitch. His dad wanted him to be a good hitter as well as a good glove man.

Billy saw thousands upon thousands of pitches. It got to the point that "Iron Mike" couldn't throw one past him.

Crack!

The batter got a hold of a pitch from assistant coach Johnny Hayes and sent the ball sailing over the head of the left-fielder.

Coach Perkins followed the flight of the ball, but suddenly he lost his concentration, and instead, he caught a glimpse of a young boy on a bicycle, disappearing from sight among the tall oak trees.

Carl knew who it was. It was now just a matter of time.

Carl Perkins knew a lot about kids. There was one fellow in town who would give him a run for his money in that regard. And that was George Thomas.

In any case, the two of them were on the same wavelength when it came to Billy Ray Reynolds.

The problem they faced: When was the best time for Billy to be presented with a Johnsonville Tigers' uniform?

Because of the situation, Carl had already added Billy to the Tigers' roster. Whether he ever played an inning or not, was not the point.

The two of them had decided if they could get him in uniform and on the bench, it would be a step in the right direction.

So, on the following Wednesday their plan went into high gear.

As usual, Billy roared down Main Street. It was 10:55 in the morning. He turned on the jets the last block and brought his bike to a screeching halt at the entrance to Cyrus's hardware store.

And like clockwork, out came Johnny, Cyrus and Carl—followed closely by a fourth member of the group, Grandpa Thomas.

Billy took one look at his grandpa and realized he was carrying a small package.

All the old-timers took a seat on the bench and waited for Billy to join them.

"Billy we got something for you," Carl said, as he took the package from George and handed it to Billy. "We want you to take this home and take a look at it. If you like what you see, we'll expect to see you at the field on Saturday morning."

Billy wasn't sure what to think, but he took the package, put it under his arm, picked up his bike and raced home.

He ran into the house unnoticed. His mother was watching the news on television. It was some news bulletin about a guy named Roger Ward, who had just won a car race somewhere in Indiana.

Billy went on upstairs. He could hear the man on television say that the car racer broke some kind of speed record of 140 miles per hour.

Billy wondered just how fast he traveled on his bike.

He closed the door to his room, sat down on his bed, and started to unwrap the box.

The box contained a baseball uniform, complete with socks and a belt. He looked at the back of the pinstripe jersey. The number startled him—it was the number "8".

That had been his dad's number throughout most of his minor league career.

And strangely enough, in his dream, the faceless figure was wearing the number eight.

Billy remembered back to what his dad had once said: "The numbers on your back don't help your batting average, but it's nice to have a favorite number. You kind of get used to it."

Eight was definitely the favorite number in the Reynolds' family. Of course, number 7 and number 9 were reserved for royalty, according to Billy's dad.

Those numbers belonged to the Yankees' M and M boys, Mickey Mantle and Roger Maris, respectively.

Billy recalled it was one summer ago when Mickey belted 54 home runs and Roger crushed 61 homers in a single season to set a major league record.

Billy was startled by a knock on his door.

He heard his mother's voice. "Billy, your grandpa is here to see you."

Billy's grandpa walked in and sat down beside him. Billy's mother looked on and watched her son's reaction to his new uniform.

"Don't you think it's time to come out from under those old oak trees and join the team?"

Billy thought to himself, "how does Grandpa know so much?"

"Cyrus ordered that uniform for you weeks ago. He's the

Tigers' number-one sponsor. He wants you to be part of the team.

"Coach Perkins and coach Hayes, too, they all want you on the team. If you want to sit on the bench, well that's okay, too. It's up to you. What do you think?"

Billy looked up at his grandpa and then looked over at his mother. He moved his head up and down, signaling his answer.

Billy thought it was time to give it a try.

Chapter 4

The Team

Carl Perkins had spent most of his adult life as a science teacher and baseball coach at Johnsonville High.

He'd loved every minute of it. He got a kick out of watching the children blossom into young men and women in just a short span of four years.

This year had been very special for his science class. He had their undivided attention for most of the year, due mainly to a couple of astronauts, John Glenn and Scott Carpenter, who both had amazed the world by orbiting their spacecrafts into deep space.

As for this year's baseball team, well, that was a different story—five wins, nine losses.

With school out and another graduating class off to make their fortunes, it was time for Carl to concentrate on his summer job: coaching the Johnsonville Little Leaguers.

Today would be the final day of practice before their season opener on Monday in Clarkson, and today, his 10-member squad was about to increase by one.

All the players were told to show up in their new uniforms. Carl had learned the hard way from previous seasons that you couldn't always count on the player's uniforms fitting snugly.

A little uniform switching among the players, or maybe, just a quick sewing job from mom over the weekend, would probably prevent a disaster.

Carl was excited about this year's team. He had everyone back from last year's team—including Willie Turner, who had won three games for the Tigers as a 10-year-old.

Unfortunately, the Tigers won only four games last season and failed to qualify for the district championship for the fifth year in a row.

Willie had a live fastball and a nice change-up last season, and, after two weeks of practice, it looked like he was throwing even harder and his change-up had a little more bite to it.

Willie was the son of Milton Turner, who was the head skycap at the regional airport. The Turners lived in Batesville, a small community ten miles west of the airport, which meant it took Milton about an hour to get his son to all the practices.

Milton was a tall man and looked to be in very good shape. According to Willie, his father was an all-state basketball player and still owns the single-season scoring record at his former high school, back in Kansas.

Carl was also lucky to have two sets of twins returning—outfielders Ryan and Michael O'Hara, along with first baseman Chucky Jameson and his brother, Jimmy, a third-sacker.

The O'Hara family moved to Johnsonville two years ago and Frank O'Hara, a businessman from Denver, bought out the only Ford dealership in town.

Ryan and Michael, both 12-year-olds, were the tallest players on the team, both measuring slightly over five-feet, eight inches tall. Ryan, who had the stronger arm of the two, played center, and Michael, who led the team in home runs last season, played right field.

As for the Jameson twins, they were the old-timers on the team. The twins would turn thirteen in September, and because of their experience, the other players voted Chucky and Jimmy this year's co-captains.

Chucky had the strongest arm of the two brothers, and he also had a knack for knocking down hard hit balls, hence, Carl had no trouble penciling him in at third base.

As for Jimmy, a lefthander, he was used to hauling in his brother's throws and was a perfect fit at first base.

The hard-nosed, tough as nails player on the team was Corky Calhoun. Corky, who had recently turned twelve, was the Tigers' catcher.

Corky grew up on a horse ranch about 20 miles outside of town. Getting bucked by a bronco was nothing new to Corky, so Carl figured he could put the youngster behind the plate and leave him there—chances are, he'd be able to handle the catching duties without a whimper.

Lenny Lockhart, the mayor's grandson, was the Tigers' second baseman and Clayton Burnside, whose dad owned the local Texaco station, was a sure-handed shortstop with excellent range, both left and right.

Lenny was a switch hitter and surprised everyone last year with his quick bat. He led the team in hits last season. Carl figured Lenny would be perfect for the number two spot in the batting order this year.

And after two weeks of practice, the most improved player from last season seemed to be Timmy Chow.

The Chow family moved to Johnsonville last spring and opened up a Chinese restaurant out by the new mini-mall.

Carl figures he's gained about four pounds since the Chow's arrival, but he is certainly happy to have Timmy on the team.

Timmy started last year batting eighth in the lineup, but by the middle of the season, Carl had moved him up to cleanup.

Timmy finished the season just three homers behind Michael O'Hara.

And the most versatile player on the team, Carlos Ramirez, was back for his third and final season.

Carlos's family owned the only Mexican restaurant in town and business was booming.

It was standing room only at Chico's on Friday nights. Chico and Teresa Ramirez knew exactly what it took to pack them in.

Carlos was the oldest of four brothers, and they all loved to play the game of baseball. In fact, Carl expects to have two of the younger Ramirez boys to be on the team next year.

Carlos shared pitching duties with Willie and Lenny last year and also gave Corky a breather at catcher. When the flu bug hit the team last season, some of the players missed a couple of games. During that stretch, Carlos played seven different positions.

All in all, Carl thought he had a pretty experienced team with eight 12-year-olds and just two 11-year-olds in Willie and Carlos—and both of them would celebrate birthdays in late July.

Billy, who turned twelve in September, would be the youngest, and shortest, on the team. Corky was the closest in size to Billy. Corky stood 5-foot-3 and tipped the scales at about 100 pounds soaking wet.

Carl liked his Tigers' chances of at least finishing above the .500 mark this season. Five wins and five losses would be quite an accomplishment, considering no Johnsonville Little League team had ever done that.

Carl figured the Tigers had an outside shot of making the championship game this season, but winning the district title—well, in the back of his mind, he figured the hair on his head was safe.

Of course, Carl would never let his Tigers hear a word of that. As far as the Tigers were concerned, Coach Perkins was going to get a "scalping".

Carl also knew his Tigers had one more important ingredient: this year's squad truly cared about each other.

Billy had watched Superman on television a dozen times. He was known as "the man of steel". It was Saturday morning, and Billy wished he could call Superman up and borrow some of that steel.

He wasn't sure he could walk down the stairs, go outside,

and jump into grandpa's jeep, much less, leap tall buildings at a single bound!

But somehow, with his glove secured tightly under his arm, he made his way out the front door. He ran across the yard and climbed into the jeep.

Billy's grandpa let out a whistle and Chipper came running and jumped into the backseat.

Billy sat back in the passenger seat and took a deep breath as his grandpa put Belle in reverse, spun her around, and headed down Fourth Street.

When George pulled into the parking lot, Billy looked over at the field. All the players were sitting on the grass in left field and Coach Perkins was standing over them, holding a clipboard.

Johnny and Cyrus were there, too. Both of them were holding bats in their hands.

There were a handful of parents sitting in the bleachers behind home plate and there were three young girls running around out in right field trying, without much success, to corral a small dog about half the size of Chipper.

Chipper barked and Billy's grandpa told him to settle down.

George had Billy follow him across the first base line, over the pitcher's mound, and out into left field to meet the team.

The collie followed at a slow trot with his tongue hanging out. He stayed as close to Billy as he could, sensing his master needed his support.

George stopped in front of the team and waited for Carl to make the introductions.

Carl moved over and put both his hands on Billy's shoulders. "Guys, I want you to meet Roscoe's grandson, Billy Ray Reynolds."

All the kids knew Roscoe and now they were meeting his grandson, the "silent one."

They would now shake hands with the pint-sized kid who would soon turn their summer into a summer they would never forget.

Carl had the team warm up.

Surprisingly, all the uniforms fit and Carl felt like all the players were happy with their numbers, their hats, and their uniforms.

They looked like a team. Of course, they hadn't played their first game of the season yet, but still, they looked like winners.

The players picked up balls from the ball bag; they gathered alongside the first base line and started to warm up their arms.

Lenny, a born politician, handed Billy a ball and said, "Do you want to warm up?"

Billy took the ball, nodded, and held the ball in his right hand. He hadn't thrown a ball for months.

It felt good. Billy put his second and third fingers across the seams, let it go, and the ball burst into Lenny's glove. The impact caused a cloud of dust to fly out of the mitt and disappear into the thin air.

Lenny took his hand out of his glove and shook it—his hand stung. At that instant, Lenny knew Billy was a ballplayer.

Lenny threw the ball back and the ball sailed over Billy's head. Billy chased the ball down, turned, and started to throw the ball back to Lenny.

Billy rubbed his eyes. He thought he saw his dad, crouched down with a catcher's mitt in his left hand, pounding his fist into the glove.

He heard his dad's voice, "Come on, Billy, throw it right here."

Stunned, Billy took a second look and then he saw Lenny motioning with his glove hand for the ball.

Billy unleashed a throw that rocketed over Lenny's head. The ball picked up speed and rolled all the way to the right field fence.

George, who was sitting in the bleachers behind home plate with Cyrus Jones, knew his grandson needed his help.

He headed for the field and kneeled down in front of Billy. Tears were flowing out of the young boy's eyes.

Johnny and Carl rushed over to lend a hand. George looked up at the two men and said, "we might be pushing it a little."

Billy and his grandpa sat down in the bleachers and watched the rest of the practice together.

And then another strange thing happened.

Billy looked out past the ball field and he thought he saw his dad's station wagon pull into the parking lot.

Billy gripped his grandpa's knee and pointed with his other hand in the direction of the station wagon.

"That's your mom, your grandma and Manny Hernandez."

Billy smiled and ran to the trio.

He hugged them all and then shook hands with his old buddy.

"Hey, amigo," Manny said. "How are you?"

Billy looked up at Manny and realized this was the day his old friend was to be in town to drop off his dad's favorite car.

George took Claire and Joan for a walk in the park to explain how Billy's first practice went, while Billy and Manny took a seat in the bleachers.

Chipper found a place to curl up near them. His ears were standing straight up as if he was trying to listen in on the one-way conversation.

Billy listened to Manny. Manny's English was very good and Billy knew that his Hispanic friend had his dad to thank for that.

Billy recalled the hours his dad had spent in the bunkhouse with Manny, going over and over as many words of the English language as he could handle.

Billy had been amazed how quickly Manny picked up the language. Billy's dad had told him once: "If you really want to learn something bad enough, you can conquer it."

Billy's dad had said Manny was a quick learner, but more importantly, it was an important goal that Manny had set for himself. He wouldn't give up, and, one day, he walked out of the bunkhouse for good, a new man, proud of himself for what he had accomplished.

Manny was certainly doing the talking now and the "silent one" was listening.

"Your dad did a lot for me and my family. I wouldn't be

talking to you like this if it hadn't been for your father. You saw how I struggled with that English book. Your father had a lot of patience with me."

And then Manny told Billy a couple of things that he had never heard before.

Manny told him of the many trips John had taken to Rancho Cordova during the off-season.

The old man proudly recalled the days when John pitched in both physically and financially, to help build Rancho Cordova's first baseball field.

"For years, the young boys and girls of Rancho Cordova had no ball field, no bats, no balls…no nothing," Manny told Billy. "Your dad provided all those things for us and somehow, he even got ahold of a used scoreboard somewhere. He fixed its electrical problems and presto, the field had its own electronic scoreboard.

"We were a very poor town and your dad made sure the kids of Rancho Cordova had a nice place to play baseball."

Manny and Billy looked out onto the Johnsonville baseball field. All the Tigers were helping the coaches put away all the equipment.

Practice was over and players would soon head home. They all hoped Billy was okay and they'd see him in Clarkson for their season opener.

Manny went on talking…

"You see Billy, you now have all this," he said, as he opened up both his hands and pointed them towards the baseball diamond. "Your dad taught you well. He taught you everything he could about the game of baseball…it was all for a very good reason. He wanted you to be the best you could be, the best baseball player you could be."

And then Manny told him something else. Billy thought it was almost as if he knew exactly what was in his head. "Your dad will always be with you," Manny said, as he placed his fist on his chest. "He's in your heart and always will be."

Billy was beginning to understand. He was beginning to put it all together. Manny hadn't been speaking English that long, but it was evident the old man had a way with words.

"I've got to catch my plane. I'm going to see my sister in California before I head back to Texas. I've got to get back to Rancho Cordova in five days. Guess what? We're having our Little League season opener at Reynolds Field."

Joan, George and Claire came back to the bleachers to say their goodbyes to Manny. They all gave Manny a big hug.

Manny leaned down and shook Billy's hand. "Adios, Billy…vaya con Dios."

They all headed for the parking lot. Chipper followed, wagging his tail.

Claire and Joan took Manny to the airport in the station wagon, while Billy, his grandpa and Chipper crawled into Belle and headed home.

It had been quite a day.

Chapter 5

Rescue at Willow Creek

By mid-morning on Sunday, the temperature had climbed twenty degrees. It was unseasonably warm for the first week of June.

George thought it would be nice to put together a picnic lunch and take Billy out to Willow Creek. Chipper could go swimming and the two of them could put their feet in the water, sit around, and have their usual one-sided conversation.

Forget the fishing, George thought to himself. The early morning would have been better for that.

Chipper and Billy were ready to go when George pulled Belle into the driveway.

Billy waved goodbye to his mom, who was busy hosing down the station wagon. George started up Belle and off they went, heading for another rendezvous at Willow Creek.

"Whew! I've never seen it so hot for this time of year," George said, as he pulled Belle into a small clearing next to Willow Creek.

Chipper was off and running.

George put the picnic basket down and found a couple of boulders with smooth surfaces, perfect for the two of them to sit on.

They took off their shoes and placed their feet in the water. The water was cool even though the sun's rays were starting to heat the boulders George and Billy were sitting on.

"Wow," George said. "These boulders are getting warm already."

The two of them sat back and watched a soggy Chipper emerge from the pond. Chipper, on a dead run, headed for the meadow and found some birds to annoy. The birds didn't hang around long as they quickly exited their resting place and flew north.

Billy turned his attention to his grandpa who was busy offering his usual words of wisdom.

George, on the other hand, could only guess what was going through the mind of his grandson, but even though he was getting older, he still had that special gift, that special ability which allowed him to actually say the right things at the right time to Billy.

As for Billy, he never stopped listening to grandpa; his grandma; his mom; and his other buddies, like Carl, Johnny, Cyrus and Manny.

Billy had taken all he had heard from them and stored the information away, much like he did when his dad offered him advice and knowledge on how to play the game of baseball.

Billy was a young boy, but he was growing up fast. He was quickly turning into a young man, and one thing was for sure, he was certainly getting all the help he needed along the way.

A strange stillness covered the pond and the surrounding meadow. Billy's grandpa stopped talking. Suddenly, Billy felt his grandpa's hands on his back and the next thing he knew, he was flying through the air and into the pond.

The coiled rattlesnake attacked quickly and jammed its fangs into George's right arm.

With his left hand, George grabbed the unwanted visitor and crushed its body with a huge rock that was next to him.

"Billy you need to get help, quickly!"

Billy got out of the water. He needed to react fast. He couldn't drive Belle. Grandpa couldn't drive Belle. He looked across the pond, and instantly, he knew what he had to do.

He quickly put on his shoes and started to run along the edge of the pond. He frantically searched for the entrance to the secret path, and, when he found the opening, he pulled back the loose brush and crawled through the hole.

He sat down and used his legs to push aside a couple of fallen tree limbs, just enough to allow Chipper to jump through the opening.

George watched both of them disappear into the bushes and at the same time he quickly took off his belt and wrapped it around the upper part of his arm.

George found a comfortable spot. He put his back against

the big rock behind him and told himself to relax and stay calm.

He looked beyond the pond one more time; he thought he heard a noise. It sounded like Chipper barking as the echo of the sound whistled through the trees. A few seconds later, the sound grew faint. And finally, he heard only the annoying sound of the crickets.

He looked up at Belle. She couldn't help him, but she sat there, proudly. When help came, they would see her first. She would shine brightly in the afternoon sun.

Johnny had told him once: "You should get one of those walkie-talkie radios for your jeep. It might come in handy someday."

George shook his head, closed his eyes, and waited.

Billy ran as fast as his legs could carry him. Chipper followed. The brush was thick and Billy would have to stop at times to clear away the debris that had fallen on the path.

Billy was frightened and there were areas of the forest that were dark and creepy, but he wouldn't slow down. He had to hurry.

The path weaved left and then right. At times, the path would come to an end, but he would quickly push the tall weeds aside and pick up the trail again.

Finally, in the distance, he could see a steady, dusty stream of light cascading through the tall trees at the edge of the forest.

He ran towards the sunlight, and suddenly, he could see the hill his grandpa had told him about.

Billy and Chipper broke into the clearing. They climbed up over the hill and ran down the other side.

Billy could see Main Street in the distance. They were almost there. Billy stumbled, slipped and fell. He rolled like a barrel, all the way to the bottom of Nob Hill. Without hesitating, he was back on his feet and on the run with Chipper close by his side.

A moment later, he could feel the cement under his feet. He ran down Main Street, pumping his arms up and down, in hopes of gaining an extra bit of acceleration that would get him to his destination sooner.

And then he saw the store...just ahead. Claire's Fountain and Drug. They had made it.

Billy and Chipper entered the drugstore. The chimes on the top of the door signaled their arrival.

A startled Claire and Joan looked up.

"Mom, Grandpa needs help!"

The words roared through the store, like they had come from heaven.

Billy's mother dropped the glass jar she was cleaning. The jar hit the floor and shattered into little pieces.

Claire hugged Joan and then put both hands over her mouth. Mr. Crane came out from behind his counter and Timmy rushed in from the storeroom.

"Grandpa got bit by a snake out at Willow Creek," Billy said. "We have to hurry!"

Joan, still in shock at hearing the words flow from her son, grabbed the cars keys and said, "Let's go get Johnny."

Johnny Hayes was sitting at his desk, enjoying a quiet

Sunday afternoon, when he looked out the window and saw Joan running across the street toward the fire station.

He rushed outside and listened to what Joan had to say. Within seconds, Joan, Claire, Billy and Chipper were nestled in the back seats of the Johnsonville fire truck as Johnny turned on the siren, pushed the accelerator to its maximum and headed out of town.

It was eight o'clock in the evening, and George opened his eyes. He was in the Grand Valley Regional Hospital and standing before him were Claire, Joan and Billy.

It was all coming back to him. He remembered he was semi-conscious when he heard the fire truck. He remembered seeing the dust swirl as Johnny wheeled the truck down the dirt road that led to Willow Creek.

He remembered Johnny applying ice to his arm. His arm had started to look more like the arm of the cartoon character "Popeye" than anything else.

Johnny had loaded him into the fire truck and in no time at all they were on the road to Grand Valley, a twenty-five mile drive—fifteen minutes at the most with Johnny putting the pedal to the metal.

He recalled looking out the back window of the fast-moving fire truck and seeing Belle, chugging down the highway at full throttle.

Claire and Joan were inside the jeep, both of them trying desperately to keep their hair out of their eyes. Billy was sitting next to Chipper, clutching his Yankee hat.

He remembered a nice nurse standing over him. "This old coot is as strong as an ox. He's going to be just fine."

The nurse placed her left hand on George's forehead and wiggled the thermometer with her other hand.

"His temperature is down," she said.

He then heard a voice he hadn't heard since last Christmas. It was the voice of his grandson.

"Hi Grandpa, I'm glad you're okay."

It was like music to George's ears. "You mean to tell me, I had to get bitten by a snake to get you talking. I was hoping to find an easier way."

Claire and Joan smiled. Billy laughed.

"You gave us a scare," Claire said. "But thanks to Billy and Johnny, the doctors and the nurses, it looks like you're going to be as good as new. In fact, it looks like you're going to be home in time."

"In time for what?" George said.

"In time to go to Clarkson, of course!"

Claire motioned to Billy. Billy walked over to his grandpa, leaned over and whispered in his ear, "I'm ready to play ball."

George Thomas had been waiting to hear those words.

"Yes!" said George, as he looked toward Joan and Claire. He clinched both fists in the air and unleashed one of those famous "Roscoe" smiles.

A knock at the door broke up the celebration and in walked Willard Smith, the sports editor of the *Grand Valley Dispatch*.

"Hello George, it's been a long time."

George looked up. The last time he'd seen Willard was back in '58 when the former freelance writer had done a feature story on baseball clowns.

"What are you doing here?" George said. "I didn't think an old man wrestling with a rattler would be newsworthy."

"You would be surprised. Sounds like a pretty good human interest story to me. As famous as you are, I wouldn't be surprised if the Associated Press picks up on it."

George shook his head and thought it was supposed to have been a nice, quiet afternoon at Willow Creek.

"Go figure."

Joan and Claire sat down in the nearby chairs and watched Willard interview George and Billy.

The two women just shook their heads. They were amazed, especially when Willard questioned Billy.

Billy talked...and talked...and talked.

Billy told Willard how his grandpa shoved him in into the pond, just an instant before the snake attacked. He told him how scary the run through the forest was and how happy he was to find his way back to town.

He told Willard about the rescue at Willow Creek, and how quickly Johnny was able to get his grandpa into the fire truck, back on the highway, and off to the hospital.

He told Willard how Belle, at full throttle, kept pace with the fast-moving fire truck with his mom, his grandmother and Chipper aboard as they all raced down the highway to Grand Valley.

Willard tipped his hat and said, "This kid can talk."

Everyone in the room laughed.

Willard said his goodbyes and headed out the door. At the same time, Dr. Ephraim Hollingsworth entered the room. "It's like Grand Central Station in here," the doctor said.

Doctor Hollingsworth walked over to the hospital bed,

glanced at George's chart and took his pulse. "I think you're a lot better off than the snake."

The good doctor explained to Joan and Claire that just as a precaution, it might be better to keep George overnight.

"If all goes well, you should be able to pick him up at eight o'clock in the morning. I understand there's a big ball game tomorrow.

"Claire, you just make sure he keeps his cool and stays put in the bleachers."

Ephraim had been George and Claire's family physician for many years, and he knew keeping *Roscoe* down was no easy task.

"We'll see to it," Claire said. "Let's all go home and let Grandpa get some rest. It's going to be another big day tomorrow."

It was going to be a great day for baseball. The sun was coming up and there were no early-morning clouds around to get in its way.

Within minutes, the sun had popped up over the mountaintops just to the east of town. The sun's bright glow signaled a brand new day for the Johnsonville residents.

Clancy Burnside unlocked the gas pumps at his Texaco station. He then found his ladder and proceeded to tie up a banner on a nearby awning. The lettering was in bright blue colors and read: Go Tigers!

In his office, the radio was blaring and a weird song was coming out of the two small speakers that hung on the wall in the garage. It was a catchy tune, but made little sense. The singer asked the question, "Who put the Bomp in the Bomp, Bomp, Bomp?"

Wally Olsen, the owner of the Johnsonville Café, was open for business. It was standing-room only, except for one revolving stool at the breakfast bar.

Eggs, hash browns and bacon were the order of the day. As for the conversations, a traveler had stopped in for a quick breakfast and had left a copy of the *Grand Valley Dispatch* behind. On the front page was a picture of *Roscoe* in his glory days.

Everyone in the café was discussing the rescue at Willow Creek.

Over at the fire station, Johnny was busy hosing down his pride and joy, the fire truck.

Johnny watched the fire truck's bright red color return as the mud and grime, picked up at Willow Creek the day before, broke off into little chunks and slid down the street, disappearing, along with a steady stream of water into the culvert at Second Street and Main.

Back over on Main Street, Cyrus Jones was busy at his hardware store, putting the finishing touches to his artwork. Using a blue crayon, he had written the words, Go Tigers, at the top of his front window and all the names and numbers of the Little Leaguers followed below, including Billy Ray Reynolds, number eight.

Cyrus walked out the front door and looked at his masterpiece. He put both hands on his hips and said, "It looks pretty good to me."

At that moment, Carl Perkins pulled up in his Chevrolet

El Camino. He came to a screeching halt, jumped out of the vehicle and took a look at his friend's handy-work.

"Nicely done, Cyrus. I see you're up early this morning."

"Yes, I guess I didn't sleep very well last night. I thought I'd get up early and come down here and get to work on this window.

"I'm worried about George. It's all over town. Have you heard anymore?"

"Yeah, I just talked to Claire. She said he was doing fine and would be getting out of the hospital this morning.

"In fact, I offered to pick him up, so I'm on my way. Put that sign of yours on the door and go with me. We'll be back before your customers come calling."

"Sounds good to me."

I don't need this old wheelchair," George said. "I can walk just fine."

"It's just hospital protocol, Mr. Thomas," the nurse said, "Now you just sit tight."

The nurse gave George a pat on the back, wheeled her former patient out the sliding glass doors, and rolled the wheelchair toward two men with dark blue baseball caps on their heads. "Well, boys, he's all yours."

Carl threw George's overnight bag in the back of the El Camino. "We'll handle him from here." George squeezed in the seat between Cyrus and Carl and the three men headed back to Johnsonville.

George was more interested in discussing Billy's miraculous recovery than he was reliving his own battle with the snake at Willow Creek.

"I'm going to be fine and it looks like we got ourselves a ball player for sure. You guys have no idea what a thrill it was to hear Billy's voice.

"His mom and Claire are so happy. They said when he ran into the drugstore and the words popped out of his mouth, they were just ecstatic. They couldn't believe what they were hearing."

Carl and Cyrus looked at their life-long friend. George was smiling. He certainly didn't look like a man who had recently tangled with a rattlesnake.

Whatever medicine Dr. Hollingsworth had given George to help in his recovery, couldn't compare to the prescription Billy had given his grandpa.

George had his grandson back...and it was time for his grandson to take the field. It was time for him to play baseball.

Chapter 6

Billy Takes the Field

The road to Clarkson during the wintertime could be tricky at times, but during the summer months, the trip was a lot more enjoyable.

The first thirty miles were uphill, straight up over the mountain. The highway would then curl its way down into a picturesque valley. Clarkson was spread out across the valley.

Travelers, coming down off the mountain, could see a water tower to the south—a big C painted on its side—and a church with a tall steeple sat on a hill to the east of town.

The town looked inviting. But when it came to Little League baseball, the town had a history of producing ball teams that would battle you to the end. Carl Perkins once said: "If you can get out of Clarkson with a win, you're doing something."

Johnsonville 3 Clarkson 1

It was two hours before game time and a steady stream of cars were heading down the mountain.

In the lead car were Carl, Johnny and Cyrus, followed by Joan, Claire, George and Billy.

Carl looked back at all the cars and said, "Looks like we're going to have quite a cheering section for our first game."

Carl turned his head, rolled down the driver's side window of his El Camino and took a peek at the little town of Clarkson, which was now just minutes away. He took a deep sigh and was thankful for the support of the Johnsonville fans.

The Tigers were in for a tough opener. Clarkson had everyone back from last year's team including a left-handed pitcher by the name of Sage Carpenter, who won six games on the mound last season and lost only two. Clarkson shutout the Tigers, 6-0, last year and Carpenter was the winning pitcher.

Carl knew they had a skilled coach in Harvey Hinton. Hinton had taken the Clarkson Beavers to the district finals four out of the last six seasons, but like the Johnsonville Tigers, they had yet to win a district title.

In fact, no team from the southern region had ever won district. That honor seemed to always stay with the powerhouses to the north, Grand Valley and Green River.

Carl had a lot of concerns about today's game. Should he save Willie for the home opener against Carbon City and start Carlos, or maybe, he should throw Lenny? Lenny was used mostly as a reliever last season, but there were times last season when he was very effective with those off-speed pitches of his.

Carl remembered one opposing player last season, telling his coach, "I can't hit that stuff."

And what about Billy? When will be the best time for Billy to get his first playing time? Maybe, Clarkson isn't the right environment for that.

First things first, Carl thought to himself, as he pulled the El Camino into the parking lot next to the Clarkson Little League field.

All his followers motored in right behind him.

The Johnsonville fans found their seats in the bleachers along the third base line and the Clarkson fans squeezed into the bleachers along the first base line.

The home team took their infield first and then it was the Tigers' turn.

Carl had Jimmy Jameson at first. At second base, Carlos Ramirez and Lenny Lockhart took turns fielding ground balls.

At third base it was Chucky Jameson warming up, and over at shortstop, it was Clayton Burnside, alternating with Billy Ray Reynolds.

Catcher Corky Calhoun was busy handling throws from behind the plate.

In left field, Timmy Chow and Willie Turner alternated catching fly balls, while Ryan and Michael O'Hara took turns running down fly balls in center field and right field.

George kept a keen eye on the pre-game warm-ups. He liked what he saw.

Coach Hayes kept hitting fly balls to the outfielders and Coach Jones did his best to corral all the throws coming in from the players.

"Cyrus has his hands full," George said, jokingly. "But I tell you what, the kids are looking pretty sharp out there."

George put his arms around Claire and Joan. "Look at that number eight, isn't he a sight."

They watched Billy as he took his turn snagging the grounders at shortstop.

"Listen," Joan said. "You can hear Billy chattering. It's such a beautiful sound."

Carl had made his decision to start Lenny. So as soon as infield practice was over, Lenny and Corky hooked up down the third base line and began warming up.

The first game of the season was fifteen minutes away.

Sage Carpenter was as advertised. He was not overpowering, but he had pinpoint accuracy.

Carpenter breezed through the first three innings unscathed. He recorded three strikeouts and forced the Tigers to ground out six times, not one ball was hit into the outfield.

Lenny, on the other hand, was as cool as a cucumber as he kept the Beavers off balance, allowing only a single up the middle to Carpenter in the second inning.

But in the top of the fourth inning, the Tigers got their first break of the game when Michael ripped a grounder through the legs of the Beavers' third-sacker. The ball rolled all the way to the left field corner and Michael trotted into second base with a stand-up double.

With two outs, Carpenter went to work on Timmy and quickly had him down in the count, two strikes to none.

But Carpenter's next offering sailed across the heart of the plate and Timmy got all of the ball and drilled it into the gap in left-centerfield.

Michael scored easily, and Timmy raced all the way home to give the Tigers a 2-0 lead.

Carpenter, visibly upset, struck out Jimmy on three pitches, and the Beavers came to bat, looking for a little revenge.

Lenny pitched well in the bottom of the fourth inning, but he did serve up a solo homerun ball to Carpenter.

Carpenter's blast—a low line drive that just barely cleared the left field fence—cut the Tigers' lead in half, at 2-1.

Both teams were retired in order in the fifth inning, but in the top of the sixth and one out, Clayton singled in the hole between third and short.

The Beavers' left fielder had trouble coming up with the ball and Clayton rounded first and set his sights on second base. He slid into second safely, but his left hand had gotten tangled up underneath the bag.

Clayton was hurt. Carl called timeout and rushed out to second base.

"It doesn't look like its broken, but let's get some ice on it and get you to the bench."

It was decision time for Coach Perkins.

Willie, who had gone in for Carlos at second base in the fourth inning, was on deck. Carlos was out of the game and that left Billy as the only replacement for Clayton.

Carl looked over at Billy. Billy walked up to Carl and said: "I'm ready, Coach Perkins."

"You're in, Billy."

Billy trotted out to second. He could hear his mother, his grandmother and his grandpa cheering encouragement from the stands.

"Go get em, Billy."

Play resumed and on the first pitch Willie hit a shot up the middle.

Billy ducked as the ball sailed over his head and bounced toward center field. And like he was shot out of a cannon, Billy raced to third. He clipped the inside corner of the bag with his right foot, and scampered home, beating the throw from the centerfielder easily as the Tigers added an important insurance run and took a 3-1 lead.

George Thomas stood up, took a moment to take in the situation, and then watched Billy run to the dugout to celebrate the play with his teammates.

"That's just beautiful," George said. "Just beautiful."

The Tigers were still not out of the woods. The Clarkson Beavers had one at-bat left and the heart of their order coming up.

Lenny was tiring, but Carl was confident his starting pitcher could go the distance. But after the first two batters reached base with back-to-back singles, the Tigers were in trouble. Carl took a deep breath as he watched Carpenter step into the batter's box.

Two runners on and no outs, and to make matters worse, the Beavers' power-hitter was up, representing the winning run. Lenny looked in and got his sign from Corky. Lenny's breaking ball curled over the plate. Carpenter took a mighty cut and drilled a line drive over the bag at second.

The Clarkson runners were off at the crack of the bat.

Out of nowhere came the Tigers' shortstop, Billy Ray Reynolds. He dove and the ball ripped into his glove. He jumped up, tagged second base and unleashed a perfect throw to first base, doubling up both runners.

A triple play!

The Johnsonville fans stormed the field. The Clarkson fans remained in their seats, stunned.

Johnsonville had won the game, 3-1. The Tigers were on their way to a season they would never forget.

As for Billy, he had finally taken the field. He had played one inning, and he had certainly made the most of it.

With one victory in the books, Carl Perkins felt like the Tigers were in pretty good shape for their home opener on Thursday against the visiting Carbon City Cubs.

The Tigers had split with the Cubs last season, and Carl had heard the Cubs had dropped their opening game, 8-0, to the Ridgedale Reds.

Unfortunately, the Tigers would be without the services of Clayton Burnside for the game. A Clarkson doctor had been on hand after the Tigers' win over the Beavers, and had taken a look at Clayton's left wrist.

"A slight sprain...not broken," the doctor said. "But he should sit out a game or two."

That, of course, left Carl with just ten players, but he did have a new ace in the hole and would have no trouble penciling in Billy at shortstop, especially after his shenanigans the other afternoon in Clarkson.

Carl was also counting on a big hometown crowd, especially with the fact the Tigers would be playing under the lights for the first time this season.

The spotlight would be on the Tigers.

Carl was right about the hometown fans. Everyone showed up—including Johnsonville bank president Jonathan Holmes, who was on hand to throw out the ceremonial first pitch.

Holmes was instrumental in getting the funding needed to upgrade the lights, upgrade the snack bar and add the extra bleachers, up and down the first and third base lines, to make it more comfortable for the fans this season.

In fact, Holmes, along with a few of the other board members, had gone out of his way to see to it that all the necessary upgrades had taken place in record time.

All of their hard work was for a good reason. Johnsonville was one of three towns in the running to host this year's District Little League championship, pitting the top team from the southern region and the team with the best regular season record from the northern division.

The crowd let out a roar as Jonathan Holmes gripped the baseball, toed the rubber, and hurled his offering to the plate, into the glove of Tigers' catcher Corky Calhoun.

Mayor Ezra Lockhart and vice-mayor Claire Thomas clapped their hands as Corky handed the ball back to Mr. Holmes.

"I think we should add him to the Tigers' roster," Mayor Lockhart said jokingly, as he motioned to Jonathan to come to the microphone, which had been temporarily set up, just to right of home plate.

"We thank you all for coming today. It's a great turnout for our first home game of the season, and now, I would like to introduce you all to Jonathan Holmes, the president of our fine bank in town, who has a special announcement to make."

"Thank you, Mayor Lockhart, and thank you vice-mayor Claire Thomas. It is my pleasure to inform you that Johnson Park has been selected as the site for this year's final game to decide the District Little League Champions.

"The game will be held on the Fourth of July—on the day we celebrate our Nation's independence. We will have our traditional parade at ten o'clock in the morning. The stock car races will start at one o'clock at the Johnsonville Raceway and the ball game will start at seven o'clock, followed immediately by our fireworks display over on Nob Hill.

"Johnsonville is known for its hospitality and has always had the reputation for putting on the best Independence Day celebration in the region. This great town loves our country and loves baseball as well. It should be a great day for all the Johnsonville residents and for all the visitors who will be in town to celebrate with us. I thank you."

Claire stepped to the microphone and thanked Jonathan as well as all the other board members for their hard work.

She then introduced the teams for today's game. First, she introduced the Carbon City Cubs as each player jogged onto the field and gathered along the third base line.

Claire then introduced the hometown Tigers, who gathered along the first base line.

The players removed their hats and sang along as the words of the "Star Spangled Banner" echoed through the loudspeakers.

Claire returned to the microphone.

"Let's play ball," she said.

Johnsonville 9 Carbon City 0

Willie Turner got the starting nod for the Tigers and the Cubs countered with right-hander Buddy Watkins, a tall, slim 12-year-old, who was getting his first pitching assignment from Carbon City coach Wallace Albertson.

Unlike the Clarkson match-up, this game proved to be a runaway for the Tigers, thanks in part to Billy's play at shortstop, the pitching of Willie, and some timely hitting from Corky and the Jameson twins, as the Tigers won easily, 9-0.

Willie tossed a two-hitter, struck out four and walked only two Cubs' hitters, while Billy threw out six runners at first base and started two double plays, hooking up with Carlos in the second inning for a twin-killing and again with the same results in the fifth inning with Lenny, who finished the game at second base.

Jimmy knocked in two runs with a double and a triple, while Corky and Chucky belted two-run homers to lead the Tigers' hitting attack.

As for Billy, he wasn't able to get the bat off his shoulder. Buddy Watkins simply couldn't throw a ball over the plate when Billy was in the batter's box.

Billy saw 12 pitches from the Cubs' right-hander and every pitch was in the dirt.

Still, Carl Perkins was pleased. After the first week of action, the Tigers were sporting a 2-0 record. The Tigers would savor their two wins for a few days, before next week's games at Ridgedale on Monday, Brighton on Wednesday and at home on Friday against Red Oak.

Except for a Saturday morning practice, Billy was free to enjoy being at home with mom and Chipper for a few days.

The Reynolds' home was now full of life. No more one-way conversations. It was all on the other end of the foot now—Billy talked most of the time, while his elders did most of the listening.

Billy biked up to the Clown's Den on Sunday after church and spent most of the afternoon with his grandpa. His grandpa told him some tall tales and Billy figured all of them were true.

Behind every picture on the wall was a story. Billy could close his eyes and George would take him somewhere— somewhere back in time.

George told him about all the trophies and how he came to own them. He told him about the glass cases and explained the story behind each individual item and their significance.

"Grandpa, what's the deal with those two?

Billy pointed first to the case with the pitching rubber in it and then to the case which contained the home plate.

"I saw Clem Allen throw a perfect game in Buffalo last year. They just happened to change pitching rubbers after the game and I was able to get ahold of the old one.

"As for the home plate, that's from an old ball park in At-lanta. The park was torn down a few years ago and I thought it would be nice to have something to remember the old park by…I clowned around at that old park many times."

George tried to pick up a ball game on the radio. "Man, there's a lot of static today. But I think I got something. I think it's a triple-A game in Oklahoma City…shucks…I lost it."

"That's okay, grandpa, we can talk some baseball. How come that pitcher from Carbon City couldn't throw me a strike?"

"Well, Billy, you're 4-feet-8 and you got that crouch in your stance. You don't give the pitchers much of a target.

"So, you're going to be facing a lot pitchers, especially the ones with very little experience, like the kid from Carbon City, and they are going to feel uncomfortable throwing to you. But believe me, your time is going to come."

"I hope so, I need a hit!"

George laughed. "Well, until you do, you just keep playing the great defense."

"I know, Dad always told me to be patient at the plate. He said 'don't swing at anything below the knees and above the chest. If you start chasing pitches, you're in trouble.'"

George agreed with that. "That's right, Billy. A keen eye, a good stance and knowing the strike zone is key. Make those pitches come to you.

"Besides, Coach Perkins told me he checked the team statistics and you're leading the team in runs scored. He's going to leave you in the leadoff spot. Your on-base percentage is one-hundred percent, you can't get any better than that."

"Grandpa, I have another question."

"What is it, Billy?"

"Do you dream?"

George was startled by his grandson's question.

"Well, of course I do. I think everyone dreams. There are good dreams and bad dreams. When I was a young boy, I had nightmares. I would dream about crazy things, but when we're growing up there is so much about life that we don't understand…sometimes, I think our mind plays tricks on us."

"I've been having a strange dream over and over again, Grandpa. When I first started having the dream I was kind of scared, but the last few times, I haven't been scared at all."

"Tell me about the dream, Billy."

"The very first time I had the dream, I saw this little figure trying to get out of a dark hole, but now when I have the dream, the hole is gone, and the figure is running across a field. There are clouds overhead and the figure is running toward something at the other end of the field, but the figure never gets any closer to what ever it is at the other end of the field.

"I hear noises, too…like a crowd yelling or something. The other night, I had the strangest dream of them all. The figure was wearing a baseball uniform with my number on it, number eight."

George was stunned. "Billy, I've had the same dream!"

"Really, Grandpa?"

George went on to tell Billy about a similar dream he has had over the past few months.

"That is strange. Billy, we're both having the same dream. Maybe, sometime in the near future, we'll be able to figure out what all this means, and when we do, it'll all make perfect sense to us."

George looked at his grandson and decided to ask him a question. "Billy, what other dreams do you have?"

"Well, Grandpa, I dream of playing baseball in the major leagues. It's the same dream my Dad had.

"I dream of being in the World Series. It's the bottom of the ninth inning and I'm at the plate. I can see the pitch as clear as day. I swing and the ball flies out of the ball park... over the left field fence.

"I feel like I'm right there. I can even smell the grass and feel the bat in my hands and can hear the crowd yelling, and then I wake up."

George smiled and said, "Now, that's a good dream...a very good dream. You hold on to that one."

Chapter 7

The Bat

Somewhere in the hills of Kentucky, Stanley Johansson was closing up shop at his bat-making plant. It had been a very long day. But, once again, Stanley, the distribution manager of the facility, had done his job. All the orders had been filled and were out the door and ready for delivery.

Stanley's desk was neat and tidy. He was about to turn off the lights and go downstairs. The workers had all left for the night, and as usual, he was the last one to leave.

It was then…he heard the noise.

The little bat fell off the shelf, hit the floor, and rolled across the room and came to a dead stop at Stanley's feet.

Stanley put his glasses on and picked up the bat. It was a Louisville Slugger all right—made from a genuine Northern white ash tree. There was no mistaking that.

But the bat was very small, too small for a major league baseball player. It was a kid's bat for sure.

Stanley noticed the branded autographed signature of the barrel of the bat. It read: *Big John Reynolds.*

Attached to the bat was a note addressed to Stanley.

Stanley,
This bat was returned to us by the parcel service. It was sent to an address in Texas, back in February, but was returned to us. Can you check it out and find out what the story is?
John, mailroom

Stanley was beside himself. He remembered he was supposed to have taken care of the little bat months ago.

In fact, he had tried to get a hold of an old friend, George Thomas, but to no avail.

George was one of those traveling baseball clowns, never in one place for any length of time, but Stanley was pretty sure George lived in southern Colorado.

Stanley was also sure George was the father-in-law of John Reynolds, who was supposed to be the recipient of the bat.

Stanley put the little bat back on the shelf. He shook his head. He recalled the sad story of John Reynolds, a very good Triple-A ball player, who hit over 150 home runs in the minor leagues, only to lose his life in a car accident just days before he was to show up at spring training with the New York Yankees.

Stanley put on his coat. He scribbled five words on a

notepad and left it on his desk. The note said: Get hold of *Roscoe.*

The next morning, Stanley left his home a little earlier than usual. He stopped in at his favorite diner for breakfast, and read, as is his normal routine, the morning paper from cover to cover.

On the back of the four-page sports section, something caught his eye. There, in the middle of the Associated Press' "around-the-world-in-sports" column, was a five-paragraph sports short about a retired baseball clown named Roscoe.

Stanley brought the page up closer to his bifocals. Wasn't this strange, he though to himself. First, the bat falls off the shelf and rolls up to his feet, and now, the very next day, he picks up a newspaper and there's a story and a mug shot of Roscoe, just the person he desperately needed to get in touch with.

The article mentioned Roscoe's real name, George Thomas, and even provided his whereabouts, Johnsonville, Colorado.

Stanley finished his breakfast, paid the bill, stuffed the newspaper under his arm and headed off to work.

In less than thirty minutes, he had made a couple of phone calls, one to the newspaper in Johnsonville, *The Chronicle*, and the other to the local drugstore in Johnsonville, *Claire's Fountain and Drug.*

Claire Thomas answered the phone. "You're calling from Kentucky and you want to talk to George Thomas?"

"Yes, I'm an old friend and I think I have something he would like to have," Stanley said, as he went on to explain the situation about the lost—and now found—little baseball bat.

Within minutes, Stanley was on the phone with George.

"Stanley Johansson! It's been a long time since I've talked to you...a couple of years at least. The last time I saw you, I was in Louisville and the Colonels had just won the pennant.

"I remember we went over to the Children's Hospital that same day and you made a bunch of kids happy...you gave them all miniature baseball bats."

"That's right George, and you had all the kids in stitches, too. I can still see you in that clown suit and I still remember those smiling faces."

"So what's up, Stanley? Are you ready to move out West to retire?"

"No, Kentucky is my home. I'm here to stay. I'm retiring in October. I finally had to break down and move into management a few years back...arthritis was setting in and I couldn't work the line anymore. I'm the head of distribution now, which brings me to the reason I'm calling."

Stanley related the story about the little bat that was having trouble finding a home...

"So, I saw the clipping in the paper with your mug on it. Aren't you a little old to be wrestling with snakes?"

George laughed. "We have a nosy reporter out here. He told me the story would make the wire services. I didn't believe it.

"As for the bat, my son-in-law ordered that bat. I remember him telling me, it was for our grandson's 12th birthday. I guess you heard the news about Big John."

"Yes, I did George. I was very sorry to hear about that."

"Thank you, Stanley. You know, it's been tough on all of us, but especially on my grandson. We would love to have that bat."

"George, I'll see to it. I'll get it forwarded to you right away. It'll probably take a week or two."

George gave Stanley the address to their box at the Johnsonville Post Office and thanked his old friend again for his help.

Billy would be in for a big surprise. George knew exactly what he was going to do. The bat would be an early birthday present for his grandson.

The Johnsonville Tigers were rolling. The Tigers devoured their next three opponents—Ridgedale, Brighton and Red Oak.

Coach Perkins had the Tigers operating on all cylinders.

With Billy at the top of the lineup, the opposing pitchers would start off a game mighty frustrated. He walked…and walked…and walked…and every now and then he'd get hit by a pitch…on the arm, on the elbow, his left foot, his right foot.

And every time Billy would reach base, he would eventually scamper home with run, after run, after run, as the heart of the Tigers' lineup would continue to knock him in.

Johnsonville 4   Ridgedale 2

Ridgedale put a scare into the Tigers early on when their hard-hitting third baseman Cubby Simpson hit a two-run homer off the Tigers' starter, Carlos Ramirez, to give the hometown Reds a 2-0 lead in the first inning.

Fortunately, Carlos settled down and shut down the Reds the rest of the way, allowing only four hits, while striking out three and walking just one batter.

In the meantime, the Tigers rallied in the top of the fourth inning. Billy led off the inning and reached base when the Ridgedale starter, Donnie Duncan, lost control of a breaking pitch. The ball grazed Billy's left arm.

Lenny walked on four straight pitches and Willie Turner followed with a three-run homer as he deposited Duncan's next pitch over the left field fence.

Clayton Burnside, who was back in the Tigers' lineup and now handling things at second base, knocked in Billy in the top of the sixth with a triple down the right field line.

Billy, who had walked with two outs in the inning, scored all the way from first for the Tigers' fourth and final run of the game.

Defensively, it was becoming very apparent that Billy, at short, and Clayton at second, seemed to be the way to go as far as Carl Perkins was concerned.

Three double plays in this game, and all three on ground balls to Clayton, who would turn and fire a strike to Billy at second base.

Billy's quick release and his relay to first base was a thing of beauty. The Tigers were becoming unstoppable up the middle.

Plus, with the Tigers' infield intact—including the James-on twins entrenched at the corners, Carl was able to keep his pitching staff, Willie, Lenny and Carlos, fresh and ready for action.

Carl was able to use his 11-man roster to its maximum, and, he was loving every minute of it.

Johnsonville 5 Brighton 0

It was the Billy and Lenny show at Brighton. Lenny won his second game of the season, hurling a two-hitter, enroute to a 5-0 shutout of the hometown Blue Jays.

Carl couldn't believe what he was seeing in this one. Billy made four diving catches to help keep the shutout intact. Billy also started two double plays. This time it was Clayton's turn to cover the bag, and both times it was a picture-perfect exchange—a real crowd-pleaser for the Johnsonville fans.

The Jameson twins supplied the long-ball against Brighton. Jimmy belted a three-run homer in the fourth and Chucky drilled a two-run shot in the fifth to complete the scoring.

Billy walked three times and scored three times. The Tigers were now 4-0, and Billy had yet to swing the bat.

Johnsonville 7 Red Oak 4

The Red Oak Orioles came to Johnsonville in hopes of knocking off the surprising Tigers, who now found themselves within one game of completing the first-round of their regular-season schedule unbeaten.

The Orioles, who had won three out of their first four games, did some damage early on and held a 4-2 lead after three innings of play.

But this time it was the heroics of Timmy Chow at the plate. Chow hit for the cycle—a single, a double, a triple and a home run, knocking in four of the seven runs.

Willie pitched four innings in this one and improved his record to 2-0 as the Tigers rallied to win the game, 7-4.

Carlos came on in the fifth and shutdown the Orioles the rest of the way to pick up the save.

Billy walked three times in the game and played superbly in the field—his fifth straight game without an error at shortstop.

The biggest defensive play of the game came in the second inning. With two outs and runners on first and second, Willie tried to throw a fastball by the Orioles' top hitter, Todd Tolleson.

But Tolleson timed the pitch perfectly and singled in the gap in left-centerfield. Ryan O'Hara cut the ball off and relayed his throw to Billy.

Billy caught the ball, turned, and then unleashed a perfect one-hop throw to Corky, who was straddling the plate, awaiting the throw.

The ball bounced into the pocket of Corky's mitt. Corky applied the tag on the lead-runner, Jimmy Johnson, for the final out of the inning.

The Orioles' coach, Wayne Chilton, shook hands with Carl Perkins after the game.

"I'll tell you one thing, Carl. This is the best Little League team you've ever had. And that shortstop of yours…well, I thought we had you on the ropes in the second inning. That was one heck of a throw to the plate."

Carl thanked the Orioles' coach. It was a nice compliment. If someone had told him the Tigers would be 5-0 at the mid-point of the schedule, he might have had that person committed.

"This is fun," Carl said out loud as he walked back to the dugout to join eleven smiling faces.

"Free pizza for everyone!"

Johnsonville 2 Clarkson 1

The Johnsonville baseball fans couldn't wait for the Tigers to play again. It was standing room only at the next home game against Clarkson.

The parking lot was jam-packed with cars. Cyrus Jones, who had just received another shipment of Tigers' hats earlier in the week, looked in the stands—everyone had a Johnsonville Tigers' hat on.

Mildred Robertson, who ran the snack bar at Johnsonville Park, had to triple her order of hotdogs and hamburgers from the local supermarket. She was afraid of running out of everything by the third inning.

Carl Perkins expected a tough game with Clarkson. The Beavers would be out for revenge. Clarkson, sporting a 4-1 record, hadn't lost a game since losing their opener to the Tigers, and the Beavers were still having nightmares—constantly reliving in their minds Billy's triple play.

The Beavers' top gun, pitcher Sage Carpenter, was a handful over at Clarkson, and Carl expected the hard-throwing left-hander to be even tougher the second time around.

Carl's strategy in this one—throw everything at them. Carlos would start. Lenny would pitch the middle innings and Willie would finish up. Three different pitchers, three different looks.

As for Clarkson, it was Carpenter all the way—and he came to play.

Aside from an opening-inning walk to Billy, Carpenter had little trouble with his control. He struck out five batters in the first three innings.

At the plate, the Beavers jumped out to a 1-0 lead in the second inning when Carlos gave up back-to-back doubles to Carpenter and the Beavers' big first baseman, Johnny Holland.

Carpenter rolled through the fourth and fifth innings, but Lenny and Willie were equally as tough—shutting down the Beavers without a hit in the third inning, the fourth, the fifth, and again in the sixth.

Trailing 1-0, the Tigers came to bat in the bottom of the sixth. Carpenter caught Clayton looking on a third strike for the first out of the inning and Chucky grounded out to third for the second out.

The Johnsonville fans cheered on the Tigers.

Carlos was up next and he hit a slow-roller up the third base line. The Beavers' third-sacker watched the ball come to a dead stop. The ball stayed in fair territory as Carlos legged out an infield single.

Billy stepped in. Carpenter tried his best to zero in on Billy's strike zone, but for the third time in the game, he walked him, putting the winning run on first base.

George, Claire and Joan stood up in their seats. The rest of the Johnsonville fans were on their feet as well.

It was up to Ryan O'Hara to keep the inning alive. O'Hara

accommodated. He hit Carpenter's first pitch down the first base line and into the right field corner.

Carlos rounded second, and then third and scampered home with the tying run. Billy was off at the crack of the bat. He blew by second base, clipped the inside of the bag at third, got the green light from third base coach Johnny Hayes and headed home.

The relay throw from the Beavers' second baseman Ricky Horton was right on the money, but Billy dove head first to the right side of home plate. His left hand grazed the plate as he slid by, a split second ahead of the catcher's tag.

"Safe," yelled the umpire.

The Tigers had done it again. Billy had done it again. The Johnsonville Tigers were a perfect 6-0.

The Tigers had earned a day off. The next game was three days away, an away game at winless Carbon City. Carl figured it was the perfect time to let the Tigers get some rest from baseball. After all, it was summertime and there were other things to do—fishing, picnicking, bicycling, roller skating, and maybe even a movie or two to see.

But Carl knew the players wouldn't forget about baseball for very long. The town would see to that.

Posters were everywhere. In the mini mall, in all the businesses up and down Main Street, at the roller rink, the bowling alley, in all the restaurants…wherever they went the kids were reminded of how popular they were.

As for Billy, his day would turn out to be a very special day.

"Billy, pick up the phone, it's your grandpa," Joan Reynolds said, as she put the turkey in the oven.

Joan had planned a family dinner for the late afternoon. Her mom and dad were coming over. It would be TV-night at the Reynolds' home. Her mom's favorite program, "Hazel", would be on television. She figured her dad and Billy might watch it, too. That's if she can keep them out of the *Clown's Den*.

Billy would be receiving a *gift* at dinner. She couldn't wait to see her son's face when he opened it.

"Hey, Billy. I'm on my way over with Belle. I've got a couple of errands to run before dinner. You want to come along?"

"Sure, Grandpa. I'll be ready."

George pulled Belle into the parking spot in front of Cyrus Jones's hardware-clothing store. Billy jumped down from Belle and followed George into the store.

"You about ready to close, Cyrus?"

"Just about, George. I see you got that hot-shot shortstop with you."

"Yeah, we're out running errands. I need some oil for that lawnmower of mine, and I also need a new rake. Mine has bit the dust."

"Coming right up, George," Cyrus said, as he glanced over at Billy, who was eyeballing the jar of sugar cookies on the counter. "Billy, are you ready for Carbon City?"

"You bet. I'm hoping to get my first hit."

"I know Billy, somebody's bound to throw you a strike one of these days," Cyrus said, as he winked at Billy and handed him a couple of cookies.

"When they do start pitching to you, they'd better watch out. You've been hitting the ball hard at batting practice. Batting off Coach Perkins and Coach Hayes is one thing, but the pitchers we've faced so far are having problems finding the strike zone with you."

"Cyrus, he's pretty frustrated," George said. "I know he's aching to get hold of one. But, I keep telling him to be patient. His time is going to come."

"Sure it will, Billy. Have you guys seen the latest statistics? Carl dropped them off this morning. Look at these," Cyrus said, as he handed George the clipboard.

"Billy, you're leading the team in walks with 13 and runs-scored with 17. That's unbelievable, you couldn't do much better than that if you got a hit every time you were up."

"Thanks, Coach Jones, but I still want a hit."

Both George and Cyrus chuckled.

"Well, Cyrus, we're off to the post office before they close. I have a very important package to pick up."

"What is it Grandpa?"

"You'll see, Billy, you'll see."

Billy noticed a tall, thin man standing behind the counter when they walked into the vacant lobby of the post office. The man was wearing a pair of big, blacked-rimmed glasses on his nose. He had a set of keys in his hands and was locking up a bunch of drawers.

"Hi Henry, you called and said I had a package to pick up."

"Sure do, George, two packages as a matter of fact," said

the senior postman, Henry Eggerson. Henry walked into the back room and came out with two cylinder-like containers.

Billy noticed one was slightly smaller than the other, but both were long and thin. They looked like they might contain a rod and reel. They were neatly wrapped and looked like they had been well-traveled.

In fact, Billy thought he saw a return address on one of them. He was able to make out the state. Kentucky! He was sure of it.

"Let's go home, Billy. We're going to be late for dinner."

Billy wanted to know what was in the packages. But his grandpa told him to be patient.

He was learning a lot about patience these days.

After dinner, the Reynolds family moved into the den. George had everyone sit down on the couch and he brought in both packages he'd picked up at the post office.

"What we have here is a present for Billy. I received a call a couple of weeks ago from a friend of mine in Kentucky. I'll read the letter he forwarded to us in a minute, but first, Billy, I want you to open the big one."

Billy tore into the package.

"Wow, it's a Louisville Slugger!" The bat was long and heavy. Billy stood up and put the barrel of the bat on the floor. The handle of the bat went all the way up to his chin.

Billy looked at the barrel of the bat. He saw the engraved signature. It was his dad's handwriting and unmistakably, his dad's signature, *Big John Reynolds*.

"It is my dad's bat." A big smile crossed Billy's face.

"Now, open this one," George said, as he handed Billy the smaller of the two packages.

Billy clawed his way through the paper as fast as he could…another bat emerged.

The bat felt like it belonged in his hands. His fingers tingled as he touched every inch of the bat from top to bottom.

Billy eyed the barrel. His dad's branded signature was on the bat as well.

Everyone looked up as George read the letter from Stanley Johansson.

Stanley explained what happened to the "little bat without a home", and he was sure it was finally in the right hands.

The final paragraphs of the letter were for Billy. George read on:

> "Billy, after my conversation with your grandpa, I made some calls and got ahold of one of your dad's bats. According to what I found out, the bat you now have was the same bat your dad used when he played in the Triple-A All-Star game in 1959.
>
> "Your dad batted twice in that game. He singled and hit a home run that was measured at 525 feet.
>
> "I'm sure you'll find a special place for your dad's bat and I also hope you get plenty of use out of your new bat as well. I'm sure your dad would have wanted you to make good use of it."
> Yours truly,
> Stanley Johansson

George put his right hand on his grandson's shoulder and with his left hand he grabbed the small bat by the handle and took a look at it.

"Billy, last Christmas I had a conversation with your dad about getting you this bat. He wanted me to check with Stanley and see if I could come up with just the right bat for you.

"Somehow, in all the confusion this little bat was lost for awhile. But, now you have it. Your dad wanted you to have it for your 12th birthday, but I think you're going to need this Louisville Slugger sooner than that.

"I know you're frustrated with all the base-on-balls this summer, but I have a feeling this little bat may have a little "magic" in it. For some unknown reason, this bat rolled off a shelf and found its way to the feet of Stanley Johannson, and now it's in your hands," George said, as he handed the bat back to Billy.

Billy rubbed his fingertips up and down the bat. He felt his hands tingle. "I think you're right Grandpa."

Billy decided to take his bat upstairs, but he was very concerned about the well-being of his dad's bat, so he asked his grandpa if he had another glass case, back at the Clown's Den, for safe-keeping.

"Sure, I do. I have just the right place for it. It'll fit perfectly right next to the others. You leave it with me, Billy. You don't have to worry."

"Thanks, Grandpa."

George, Joan and Claire watched the young man head upstairs. Billy held the bat tightly as he made his way up the steps.

While his elders settled in to watch the latest episode of "Hazel", Billy was busy in his closet upstairs. He placed the bat in his secret hiding place. There was plenty of room, right next to his boxes of baseball cards.

The bat was safe. It had been a great present. Billy ran downstairs and joined his family.

He looked up at the ceiling. He thought he heard something rattle up stairs. It was probably his imagination.

Chapter 8

The Monster at Green River

"Ryan and Michael have the mumps!"

Carl was flabbergasted.

On the other end of the phone call, it was Frank O'Hara, relaying the bad news to the Tigers' coach.

"The doctor said another week to ten days. The boys are disappointed, but we need to keep them quarantined and away from the rest of the team.

"Otherwise, you could have a catastrophe on your hands. We'll get them back out there as soon as they're over the hump and not contagious anymore."

"Thanks, Frank. Tell the boys to hang in there and tell them we're thinking about them."

Carl hung up the phone. He shook his head. He knew the Tigers' unbeaten streak was now in jeopardy. But, more importantly, the road to the District Championship was now

full of potholes, one slip-up and the Tigers could be specta-
tors on the Fourth of July.

The Tigers had four games left and they needed to win
two of the games to clinch a spot in the final.

With just nine players, the Tigers would have their work
cut out for them. One injury—like the wrist injury to Clayton
earlier in the season, a parent failing to get their son to the
game on time, a hitting slump—you name it, any number of
things could ruin the Tigers' chance at a title.

Carl Perkins needed to get all those negative thoughts
out of his head. The Tigers needed to focus on one game at a
time. Carl would need to get that across to his players.

Carl picked up the Tigers' roster from his desk, picked
up the phone and called every parent, setting up a special
practice and a special meeting with the parents the next
morning.

It was just after midnight. Billy had been asleep, when
suddenly the dream appeared. This time, the dream had
taken on a strange twist.

*There was never a black hole. It was a dugout! Billy could see
it clearly, now. The figure took three steps and emerged out of the
dugout and into the bright sunlight. The figure turned and re-
vealed its face—it was Billy.*

*Billy moved to the on-deck circle. He kneeled down. He clutched
the Louisville Slugger by the handle, tightly, with both hands.*

*He looked out toward the outfield. Out of nowhere, clouds ap-
peared. The clouds stayed low to the ground. Lights appeared, first
in left field, then in center field, and finally in right field.*

The glow from the lights and the low-hanging clouds created an eerie feeling. Suddenly, the clouds disappeared and a huge figure emerged from the shadows of the lights. The figure was wearing a green uniform and it was on the move, heading for the pitcher's mound. There was white lettering on the jersey, but Billy couldn't quite make out the words.

Billy looked at his hands. The bat was gone. He looked up...the figure in the green uniform was gone. It was then he heard the rattle. He was in bed! The covers were wrapped around his shoulders. He pulled his body over toward the edge of the bed. There, on the floor was his bat—rolling back and forth. His dad's branded signature was the last thing he saw.

"Wake up, Billy, it's time for breakfast," Joan yelled from the bottom of the stairs. "Coach Perkins called, you have a special practice this morning."

Startled, Billy glanced at the floor. He jumped down and looked under the bed. He bolted for the closet, pulled back the slats...and there...next to the boxes of baseball cards was his Louisville Slugger right where he left it.

Billy took a deep breath and covered up his hiding place. "I've got to tell Grandpa about this."

Billy sat on the swing. Chipper was sprawled out on the porch. They both waited patiently for Belle to roll into the driveway.

George placed the palm of his right hand on the center of Belle's steering wheel. The horn beeped twice, and Billy and Chipper ran off the porch and jumped into the jeep.

Before they reached Johnson Park, Billy, without taking a deep breath, informed his grandpa of his latest dream.

"Grandpa, you didn't have the same dream last night, did you?"

"Oh, yes I did, Billy. Mine was a little different. I saw those same clouds, the lights, and the monster in the green uniform. But, I didn't have a Louisville Slugger rolling around at the edge of my bed.

"I'm sure there's a good reason for our crazy dreams. But I know one thing for sure. You're taking that bat of yours to Carbon City."

George pulled Belle into the parking lot at Johnson Park. Billy looked over at the ball diamond. He saw all his team-mates' parents heading for the bleachers. "I wonder what's going on, Grandpa?"

With Cyrus and Johnny as his side, Carl had the players and all the parents take a seat in the bleachers behind home plate and proceeded to inform them of the bad news.

"The good news is we still have enough players to field a team. We are currently in first place and need just two more wins to secure a spot in the district finals.

"As for you parents, it's imperative that you get the kids to the remaining games on time. One slip up, we forfeit. And we don't want that to happen."

All the parents shook hands with Carl and the coaches. They all promised to do their part.

Milton Turner, Willie's father, was the last parent to leave the bleachers. "Coach Perkins, don't worry about a thing. This has been such a great season and we don't want to up-set the apple cart. I promise you, I'll have Willie on time... every time."

"Thanks, Milton. I know you have a long way to come to make the games and the practices. That's just the kind of support we need."

"We have the greatest parents, the best fans, and the best team we've ever had in the history of the Johnsonville Little League. With everyone's help, we can do this."

With the meeting over, Carl was now free to talk to his players—his nine players one-on-one.

Billy and his teammates knelt down in front of their coach and listened. "This is what we're going to do."

Johnsonville 8 Carbon City 0

Billy sat in the dugout and watched Carbon City's starting pitcher, Buddy Watkins, head for the mound.

The last time Billy faced Buddy he saw nothing but balls in the dirt. Billy moved to the on-deck circle and watched the Cubs' right-hander finish his warm-up pitches.

Billy noticed Buddy's delivery was a lot better. Every one of his pitches were right over the plate. Just maybe, Billy thought, this would be the day he would finally get the bat on the ball.

Billy looked toward the visitors' stands. His grandpa gave him the "thumbs up" sign. Billy grabbed his new bat by the handle. He waved to his grandpa, his grandma, and his mother. All three stood up to cheer him on.

Joan said, "Look at those dimples. Oh, what a sight to see. Mom and Dad, I have the strangest feeling something good is going to happen."

Billy stepped into the batter's box. He planted his right foot in the far corner of the box and took his stance.

The umpire yelled, "Play ball!"

The first pitch was in the dirt. George shook his head. Joan and Claire put their hands in the air as if to say, "Here we go again."

On the very next pitch, a gust of wind crossed home plate, just as Buddy let go of the ball. The ball was heading for the outside of the plate, too far for Billy to take a cut at, but the wind brought the ball back over the plate.

Billy swung. Billy connected.

The ball sailed over the head of the Cubs' shortstop, Timmy Tuttle. It was a "tweener". The ball rolled past the outfielders and didn't stop bouncing until it banged up against the fence in left-centerfield.

Billy was off and running. He shot out of the batter's box. He rounded first base, then second, and was in standing up at third base with a booming triple.

Carl Perkins stood up. "That's what we needed."

Billy raised both his arms in the air.

He had his first hit.

There would be no stopping the Tigers. Lenny followed with a single up the middle to score Billy, easily. Willie doubled. Timmy followed with his third homer of the season as the Tigers jumped out to a 4-0 lead.

The Tigers scored two more runs in the fifth and two more in the sixth enroute to an 8-0 win. Carlos pitched six innings of shutout ball, striking out three and walking only two.

Billy made two diving catches at shortstop and teamed up, once again, with Clayton for two more double plays— the duos seventh and eighth twin-killing of the season, as the Tigers improved to 7-0 to keep their unblemished record intact.

The Johnsonville fans stood up, applauded the Tigers and headed for the parking lot. The ride back to Johnsonville would be a joyful one for all.

George, Claire, Joan and Billy climbed into the Crown Victoria and headed home.

Billy sat in the back seat. He was a happy camper. Billy had walked three times in the game, but his lead-off triple had broken the curse. He was batting a thousand. One for one!

"How do you feel, Billy?" George said.

"I feel great Grandpa. I couldn't believe that pitch in the first inning. It looked like it was going to be outside and all of a sudden it came right over the plate."

"It was a great hit," Claire said.

"It was just wonderful," Joan said as she squeezed her son's cheeks. "It is nice to see those cute dimples, too."

"Ah, Mom," Billy said, as he looked down at his bat. He put his mitt over the handle and placed the palm of his right hand over the knob of the bat.

Once again, he felt his hands tingle.

He replayed the first inning in his head, all over again. It was a feeling he wanted to have again, soon.

Johnsonville 5 Ridgedale 2

Johnsonville 6 Brighton 1

Despite having just nine players, nothing seemed to stop the surging Tigers as they continued to win, knocking off

Ridgedale, 5-2, and Brighton, 6-1. Both games were at home in front of their home crowd.

Carl Perkins had moved Timmy to center field and decided to rotate his pitching staff—Carlos, Willie and Lenny—to left field and center field to fill the void with the absence of the O'Hara twins.

Whatever Carl came up with seemed to work. It seemed like nothing could stop the Tigers.

Billy, all of a sudden, was getting pitches to hit. He was 2-for-2 and a walk against Ridgedale. He singled, doubled and tripled in three at bats against Brighton.

All the hits were ropes—either shots up the middle or hard hit balls down first or third base lines.

He was a terror on the field as well. With nine games in the books, Billy had yet to make an error and he had teamed up with Clayton for a total of 12 double plays.

Johnsonville 2 Red Oak 0

By the time the Tigers headed for Red Oak for the regular season finale, they had already clinched a spot in the district final and were on the verge of completing their regular season unbeaten.

The Orioles would like nothing better than to knock off the high-flying Tigers. The Orioles, like everyone else in the southern region, were in the "wait until next year mode", but the Red Oak team had enough talented players to make the game very interesting.

Red Oak would finish third in the standings, behind Johnsonville and Clarkson, but they did have Todd Tolleson, their top pitcher at 3-1, and their top hitter with a healthy .400 average.

Willie, 3-0, would get the starting nod for the Tigers in this one.

Both pitchers settled into a pitching duel early on as Todd allowed only one runner to reach first base during the first three innings.

Billy was hit by a pitch to open the game, but was left stranded at first when Todd came right back to strike out Lenny, Willie and Timmy to get out of the inning.

Willie countered, allowing only a single up the middle to Todd in the second inning.

In the top of the fifth, Corky reached base on an infield hit and Carlos walked. With two outs, Billy stepped to the plate.

He settled in, hoping to get a pitch to his liking. Once again, Billy felt a slight breeze. Dust blew across the infield. Billy picked up the pitch quickly as it left the right arm of Tolleson.

The pitch was inside, but Billy got around on it and ripped a shot down the line and into the left field corner. Both runners scored and Billy went in standing up at second base with a double.

The Tigers were up, 2-0. Billy had come through with another clutch hit. The Tigers needed just six more outs to go 10-0.

Willie was in complete control the rest of the way. He struck out five of the last six batters, fanning Todd Tolleson on three straight pitches for the final out of the game.

Gloves were in the air. The Tigers jumped for joy. George

was out of the bleachers and was the first to shake hands with Carl Perkins.

"What an amazing season. There's going to be a lot of fireworks on the Fourth of July."

"Hi guys. Can I have a moment of your time?"

George and Carl looked around.

Standing next to them was Willard Smith.

"Willard, what are you doing here?"

"It looks like the Johnsonville Tigers deserve a headline or two in the Grand Valley Dispatch. Don't you think?"

"Well, I guess they do," George said.

Carl agreed. "That's Carl Perkins with a C," the Tigers coach said as he shook hands with the reporter.

"George and Carl with a C, I'm also here for another reason. I'm going up to Green River tomorrow to cover a game.

"It might be of interest to both of you to come along. George, you're welcome to bring your grandson along, too. I've got plenty of room. You might find the game very interesting."

"I think we can make it," George said.

"Good," the reporter said. "Meet me at the paper, say three o'clock. I'll drive from there."

"See you then," George said.

George and Carl knew what was up. They were going on a scouting expedition. They would soon get a good look at the Tigers' next opponent—the team they'd be facing for the District Championship.

And thanks to Willard, they would be using his gas to get there.

George had a feeling Willard had a lot more to tell them. George was sure there was a lot more to the story...

George, Carl and Billy pulled into the parking lot adjacent to the building that housed the Grand Valley Dispatch. The newspaper was the only daily paper in the region and, thanks mainly to the efforts of Willard Smith, it had an award-winning sports section, providing coverage to the entire region.

Willard was waiting for them in the lobby.

"Hi, guys, you're right on time."

Willard picked up his briefcase, stuck the current edition of the "Dispatch" under his arm, and led his friends from Johnsonville back out to the parking lot and into his Ford station wagon.

It would take Willard a little over an hour to get to Green River, plenty of time to enlighten his guest travelers on the latest news in the sports world—the world involving a 200-mile radius of Grand Valley, that is.

Willard made a right turn out of the parking lot, took a left at the next light and then a quick right onto the on-ramp, which led up over a hill and eventually on to the interstate.

He handed Carl a copy of the Dispatch, reached in his briefcase and pulled out another one, tossing it to George, who was sitting in the back seat with Billy.

"Take a look, there will be a question and answer period later," Willard said, jokingly.

Both men went right to the sports page.

The first headline that caught their eye, read: Johnson-ville qualifies for District Little League Championship.

"Look, Billy. There's a picture of our team celebrating af-ter the Red Oak game," George said. "There's a picture of you when you back-handed that grounder in the second in-ning."

"Cool, Grandpa." Billy said, as he leaned over to get a view of the rest of the article.

"That's a nice story, Willard. You talk about our unde-feated season and everything," Carl said. "You devoted a whole page to the Tigers. That's really nice."

"You better turn the page," Willard said. "You're going to find the next page very interesting."

The headline on the next page, read: "Boomer McPher-son tosses perfect game; strikes out 15 as Green River de-molishes Henderson, 10-0."

"Who the heck is Boomer McPherson?" Carl said.

"You guys better read on," the reporter insisted.

George read fast. The Green River Rats would be the Ti-gers' final opponent. George realized rather quickly that the Tigers were not the only unbeaten team in the region.

"Is that a picture of their coach?" George said.

"No, it isn't, George. Read the caption. That's Boomer McPherson, he stands 6-feet-1 and weighs 200 pounds."

"Has anyone checked his birth certificate?" Carl said, as he took off his Tigers' hat and rubbed his brow with his right forearm.

"He's legit. He's a farm boy. The oldest son of Joel McPher-son," said Willard. "There's four boys and they all play for the Rats."

"What the heck are they feeding them up there?" said George, as he handed the sports page to Billy.

Billy looked at the picture of Boomer McPherson. Billy couldn't takes his eyes off the photo. There was something eerie about the picture…

Willard kept his eyes on the highway, but that didn't stop him from talking. The reporter knew everything there was to know about Boomer McPherson and the Green River Rats.

They had won eight of their nine games by the mercy-rule. They took no prisoners; that was the bottom line. The only team to even score on them was Grand Valley.

"I thought the Grand Valley Giants had the best team in the northern region until the Rats showed up three weeks ago and walked away with an 8-1 victory. I think they picked up their only run in the final inning, long after Boomer McPherson had retired to the dugout," continued the reporter, as he rolled on down the highway.

By now, Billy was listening to every word out of Willard's mouth. He finally took his eyes away from the newspaper. He saw a green sign flash by—Green River, 35 miles.

Willard said the Giants would get another shot at the Rats tonight. But even if Grand Valley could pull off the win, they'd still finish second in the northern region, due to the fact they already had two losses—their other loss coming to Cameron, 4-3, last month.

Willard was also quick to admit that he was a sportswriter, not a fortune teller, but if he was to change professions just for tonight, he certainly wouldn't have any problem predicting the outcome of the game.

"Boomer has pitched just four times. He's thrown two

perfect games and has yet to allow a hit...not one hit. He's walked maybe four or five batters all year, and that's because that blazing fastball of his will take off on him."

"My goodness, when Boomer and the Rats came to Grand Valley, I saw him unleash a throw over the head of the catcher. The ball ripped into the backstop and tore a hole right through the webbing."

"Gee, Willard," said George. "Can you give us some good news?

"Well, I guess I can. Defensively, your guys may have the upper hand. I think you have a little more speed on the bases and, of course, you'll have the home field advantage. Unfortunately, someone will have to get to Boomer, and so far, nobody has come close to even fouling a pitch off."

George put his arm around Billy and pointed to the highway sign: Green River City Limits.

"This is a poor town," Willard said, as he took a right and then a left and headed to the south end of town. "The ball field is nothing like what you guys are used to. It's no Johnson Park. In fact, it's a dirt field. The lights flicker once in a while, and I've seen many outfielders spend a moment or two picking up pebbles before the start of a game."

Willard went on to give them a rundown on the history of Green River. A few years back Green River was booming. The population doubled almost overnight as oil companies moved in. But after a few years of drilling and a lot of behind-the-scenes political problems, the oil companies were gone, taking with them half the residents and half of the businesses.

"It's a tough town now," Willard continued. "As for the

Green River Rats, they are a tough bunch of kids. Boomer and his brothers: Bugs, Bumper and Booker T, all smack the ball. The locals call them the "Rat Pack". They bat second, third, fourth and fifth in the lineup, and the opposing pitchers cannot take a breath until they maneuver their way through those four."

Willard turned on his windshield wipers. "I can't believe this, every time I come up here it rains. It looks like a pretty good storm is brewing."

The reporter pulled into a muddied parking lot. The rain had stopped as quickly as it had started. Both teams had returned to the field to warm up. Willard, George, Carl and Billy found seats in the bleachers behind home plate.

The umpires had gathered at home plate with coach Filo Hamilton of the Rats and coach Charlie Wilson from the Grand Valley Giants.

Billy overheard the head umpire tell the coaches, "I'm not sure we can get this one in. Filo, get your kids on the field and let's give it a shot."

Suddenly the lights came on. Billy noticed the lights were not very bright; there were shadows in the outfield and there were a few low-lying clouds moving in from centerfield.

And then Billy saw him. Boomer McPherson came out of the dugout and headed for the mound. Billy grabbed his grandpa's arm.

"That's him Grandpa. That's the monster in my dream."

Boomer took off his jacket...the jacket was riddled with rain drops. The white lettering on his uniform read, "Green River Rats."

"I know, Billy, I see him," George said, as he looked

around for the whereabouts of Willard, who was now at the bottom of the bleachers talking to Carl Perkins and another reporter. "Let's keep this between us. We don't want Willard to think we're crazy. No telling what would show up in tomorrow's paper."

"I got you, Grandpa. But just look at that kid. Look how big he is!"

"Billy, everyone on this team is big. Look at those outfielders, they're bigger than the O'Hara brothers. They look more like a high school team than a Little League team."

Boomer toed the rubber, but before he could unleash his first warm-up pitch, lightning struck the fence in left field. The storm had made a u-turn and was back with a vengeance.

"That's it," the umpire said. "There will be no game tonight. The fans scurried back to their cars. The players ran for cover in the dugouts. George, Carl and Billy followed Willard back to his station wagon and jumped in just seconds before the next bolt of lightning struck the fence in right field.

"It looks like a war-zone out there," George said.

Willard rolled down his window as he caught a glimpse of Filo Hamilton and his son, Ronnie, jump into a pickup truck.

"Filo, I guess the game is history."

"Yeah, they called it," Filo said. "It doesn't matter, we won the region title anyway. I guess we'll see you down in Johnsonville. We're just one win from the District Championship. We've pretty much crushed all our opponents. I figure we shouldn't have a problem beating that team down there. You'd better save us plenty of space in the paper."

"Oh, I will, Filo…I will."

Willard rolled up the window and said, "He seems like a pretty confident fellow."

George, Carl and Billy kept quiet most of the way back to Grand Valley. They were a captive audience. Willard spent most of the time talking about the McPherson brothers, and especially Boomer.

It was a tall tale and before Willard was through, the three of them actually felt sorry for the McPherson brothers.

Supposedly, the boys were up at the crack of dawn everyday—baling hay, milking cows, and shoveling manure. Then they'd walk two miles to school, and two miles back.

At least, they had their late-afternoons free to play ball in the back pasture. It wasn't long before they realized just how fast Boomer could throw a ball. Bugs was the catcher of the group and rumor has it, he spent his late evenings in bed, re-stringing his catchers' mitt.

George, Carl and Billy were glad when Willard pulled into the parking lot of the Grand Valley Dispatch. They shook hands with Willard, said their goodbyes and headed back to Johnsonville.

It had been a very interesting afternoon.

George rubbed the back of Billy's neck and glanced over at his friend, Carl, who had both hands on the steering wheel of his El Camino, as the three of them rolled down the state highway.

"Carl, you look a little pale," George said. "You shouldn't believe everything that comes out of Willard's mouth. His articles in the newspaper are pretty factual, but sometimes when he tells his tales, it's hard to separate fact from fiction."

"Yeah, I kind of figured that. But, he told me a couple of tall tales about the "Rat Pack" that were very interesting."

"Like what? George questioned.

"Well, I guess the story goes, Boomer and Booker T are their real names all right...says right on their birth certificates, but Bugs and Bumper, those are nicknames. Their real names are Frederick and Gerald. I guess both of them picked up those "handles" last year, during their first year of Little League.

"Supposedly, Bumper has a habit of falling down a lot and bumping into people. He's the most accident-prone of the brothers. As for Bugs, well, Willard made me laugh when he told me this one."

Billy was intrigued. "Coach Perkins, what did he say about Bugs?"

"Well, Billy, it seems Bugs has a habit of running the bases with his mouth open. Last year during the the Rats' season opener he hit a triple, but on his way to third he encountered a handful of bugs, all of which decided to take refuge down his throat."

"What happened then? Billy said.

"Oh, he made it to third all right. He called time out and had a little coughing spell. He later scored on a base hit by one of his brothers, but the nickname stuck with him from that day forward."

Billy laughed.

"Yes, that's a cute story, but there's nothing funny about the "Rat Pack". I think they're for real. As for Boomer McPherson, that kid's a monster."

"No, he's no monster," George said, as he winked at Billy. "He's a dream come true."

Chapter 9

The Parade

It was the second of July, two days before the fireworks would start. Two days before the parade and the big Fourth of July celebration, and two days before the big game—the game that would decide the District Little League Championship.

Mayor Ezra Lockhart's phone was ringing off the hook. The vice-mayor, Claire Thomas, was in the front office handling most of the calls and, at the same time, was working with parade coordinator, Lilly Thompson, trying to make sense out of all the paperwork involving all the entrants in the Johnsonville Fourth of July Parade.

"Hey girls, guess what?" Mayor Lockhart said. "I just hung up the phone with Frank O'Hara. He's been so kind to lend us four new trucks for the parade—two for our Tigers and two for the Green River Rats."

"That's wonderful," Claire said. "The kids deserve it. They'll get a kick out of it."

"Are we all set with the floats?" Claire asked Lilly.

"Let's see, it looks like twenty floats in all. We just confirmed two more. The Chow House entered a float with a Chinese theme and the Ramirez family over at Chico's will have a float with a Mexican theme, complete with mariachis."

"That sounds very colorful," Claire said. "Sounds like we're all set, Lilly. We have four bands that called today and reconfirmed.

"Let's see. We have the Johnsonville High School band, the Grand Valley High School band, and the local Elks Club has entered a 20-piece Dixieland-style band.

"I also had a call an hour ago from a John Johnstone, up in Green River. He's a part-time music teacher at the high school up there, and they have a small 30-piece marching band that they want to bring down."

"Sounds like we're all set," Ezra said. "Cyrus Jones and all the business owners along Main Street and down First Street will have their places decorated to the hilt. It's going to be a great day."

Claire looked at her watch and grabbed her purse. "Well, guys. Let's close up shop. I need to close down the drugstore and get home. Billy and Joan are coming over for dinner. In fact, they're probably there now. Billy is probably having a ball helping George put the finishing touches on Belle."

Joan Reynolds looked out her mother's kitchen window. She had fried chicken sizzling on the stove. Her mother would be home soon. The family would be having dinner together tonight and discuss the events which were to take place in the next forty-eight hours.

She saw Billy and her dad push Belle out of the carport and into the driveway. Belle had changed from her familiar military green to a beautiful red, white and blue.

George had explained to the family a few weeks back that Belle would be coming out of retirement for one last parade—she would be the lead car in Johnsonville's Fourth of July Parade.

She smiled as she watched Billy use a rag to clean Belle's windshield, headlights and taillights. It was a good afternoon for Billy. For a few hours anyway, her son had the chance to think about something other than baseball, the big game...and Boomer McPherson.

George had also explained to the family that he would be coming out of retirement. Roscoe would be making one more appearance. One more time he would hop on Belle and put on a show.

This time, he would let Billy pick out the costume. Out of the hundreds of colorful costumes in the Clown's Den, it would be Billy's decision to come up with just the right one.

"Billy, I think Belle is ready for the parade," George said.

"She looks great Grandpa."

"Let's push her back into the carport. We need to keep her nice and clean."

With Belle safely back in her parking spot, George put his right hand on Billy's shoulder. "We need to go back into the Clown's Den. You have a decision to make."

Billy ran inside and looked up at all the costumes. "Gee, I don't know, Grandpa. There are so many."

"I'm sure you'll find the right one, just take your time."

Billy looked and looked. And then he saw it. Up in the very top left-hand corner of the room. "That's it, Grandpa. That one, right there."

George grabbed the ladder. He took a few steps up the ladder and unhooked the costume. It was red, white, blue.

"That's 'Uncle Sam'. I've used this one many, many times," George recalled. "I better have your grandma look at the pants. They may be a little tight around the waist, but this costume is the right choice, Billy. Belle and I will certainly get the crowd's attention. We'll have plenty of red, white and blue."

George glanced at the clock on the wall. Claire should be home and Joan is probably about ready to call in the troops for dinner.

"Billy, we'd better wash up, it's time for dinner."

Billy was on his second chicken leg and his second helping of mashed potatoes when the conversation turned to Boomer McPherson and the Green River Rats.

"Billy, Grandpa said you got a pretty good look at the competition up at Green River. How do you think you and the Tigers are going to do against the Rats? Claire asked.

"We're going to win," Billy said. "We are going to beat them."

"George, I thought you said the Rats were undefeated and they had a pitcher that was a foot-and-a-half taller and outweighed Billy about 120 pounds!"

"I, did."

"I thought you said most of the players had facial hair and looked more like a high school team than a Little League team!"

"I, did."

"I thought you said this Boomer McPherson kid had thrown two perfect games this year and has yet to allow a hit!"

"I, did," said George one more time. "And that's all true, but we have a secret weapon."

"What secret weapon, is that?" Joan quizzed.

"We have Billy Ray Reynolds!" George said.

Joan and Claire smiled and looked across the table at Billy. George put his thumbs up and grinned.

Billy said: "Will someone please pass the mashed potatoes?"

It was seven o'clock in the morning, the Fourth of July. It would turn out to be the most exciting day in the young life of Billy Ray Reynolds.

Billy, surprisingly, climbed out of bed refreshed. Coach Perkins had put Billy and the rest of the Tigers through a two-hour workout the day before—their final "tune-up" before the championship game.

Billy had gone to bed early. The first step in preparation for the game was to get a good nights sleep. He had done that. He had slept straight through—no dreams of black holes and monsters in the outfield. He had faced his dream front and center just days before. Now it was time to face the future. The conclusion of his dream was just hours away.

Before he had gone to sleep, he took his Louisville Slugger from its hiding place and placed it next to his bed. He also took some of his baseball cards out of the boxes and shuffled through them. He had some of the best cards in the world. He had Mickey Mantle and Roger Maris of the Yankees, Duke Snider and Pee Wee Reese of the Dodgers, Willie Mays from the Giants, and Stan Musial from the Cardinals.

Billy thought to himself. All those great players had obstacles to overcome. They probably had faced guys like Boomer McPherson plenty of times when they were growing up.

If Billy's goal was to make it to the "Big Show" someday, he would need to conquer the likes of a Boomer McPherson over and over again.

This was just the beginning. Billy felt he was ready to face the "Rat Pack". He was ready to lead his teammates into the game of their young lives.

It was a beautiful day for a parade...and a beautiful day for baseball. It was nine o'clock in the morning and the parade route was already jam-packed with people.

There were vendors selling cotton candy, peanuts and popcorn. There were kids everywhere. Visitors had come from as far away as Denver and Grand Junction.

All the town leaders were out and about. Banker Jonathan Holmes was there. Mayor Ezra Lockhart and vice-mayor Claire Thomas were walking the streets and shaking hands with everyone.

Gas station owner Clancy Burnside, barber Ted Carrillo and café owner Wally Olson—all had ringside seats, and were waiting patiently to see the arrival of "Roscoe" and the start to the parade.

The Jameson family—including Robert and Betty and their two daughters, Sheila and Suzanne—squeezed into a spot across from Claire's drugstore in hopes of catching a glimpse of Chucky and Jimmy.

Milton Turner and his wife, Elsie, found a nice viewing area, just a half a block from Cyrus' hardware store, and Corky Calhoun's parents, Matthew and Corinne, backed their pickup in front of Clancy's garage, spread out a blanket in the bed of their truck, and waited patiently for Roscoe and Belle to turn the corner.

Frank O'Hara and his wife, Charlene, found a spot on First Street. The O'Hara's, who were happy parents now that their two boys were free of the mumps and would be back on the ball field today, had their cameras turned on and in the "ready" position.

Parade coordinator Lilly Thompson picked up the microphone and she stood atop the temporary bandstand, which allowed her a bird's eye view of Main Street. "Here they come…ladies and gentlemen…welcome to the 1962 Johnsonville Independence Day Parade".

Belle rolled down the street in her glory. Roscoe waved to the crowd. He then pulled back a tarp and unleashed hundreds of red, white and blue balloons that sailed upwards into the bright blue sky.

Roscoe pulled Belle to a stop. He got out, danced around the jeep—showing off his over-sized shoes and a bright, red curly-top wig. He shook hands with every kid on the block, threw kisses to the crowd, jumped back into Belle, honked her horn a few times and rolled on down the street.

The Johnsonville High School band followed. The bandleader, high school senior Travis Johnson, gave his signal and the band bellowed out the Star Spangled Banner.

The colorful floats followed, including the Ramirez family on an eight-wheeled flatbed truck. Three teenage couples were performing the Mexican hat dance, while eight mariachis, with their guitars blazing, kept in step—as they made their way down the street.

The Chow family turned the corner and the O'Hara's were quick to take pictures. The Chow's had gone all out to give the parade onlookers a quick view of their Chinese heritage. On the six-wheeled trailer were Timmy's three sisters—Jenny, Gwen and Gloria—decked out in beautiful costumes. At the far end of the float stood Timmy's grandfather, Henry, holding a giant drum and keeping time to the music as they rolled on down the street.

Moments later, Frank O'Hara's Ford trucks turned the corner. Carl Perkins was driving the first truck, Cyrus Jones was at the wheel of the second.

Billy, Willie, Lenny, Carlos and Timmy were sitting in the bed of the first truck, waving and acknowledging the cheers from the crowd. The Jameson twins, the O'Hara twins, along with Corky and Clayton, smiled to the crowd and waved their Tigers' hats as Cyrus maneuvered the second vehicle slowly down the street.

Green River's 30-piece marching band—playing a catchy blues tune—separated the two teams as the next two trucks followed—driven by Frank's top two salesmen of the year, Lawrence Smith and Bill Boyles.

Sitting next to Lawrence Smith was the Green River Rats' coach, Filo Hamilton, giving a "thumbs up" to the crowd as they passed by. In the back of the truck were Boomer, Booker T, Bumper and Bugs, along with Filo's son, Ronnie, and Woodrow Harrington, the Rats' only other starting pitcher.

Frank O'Hara removed the camera from his eyes and looked over at his wife. "Honey, is it my imagination? It looks like the tires are flat on that third truck?"

"No, Dear," she said. "But there are some big boys in the bed of that truck!"

Bill Boyles followed closely behind his buddy, Lawrence. He thought to himself and then said out loud: "It looks like Larry's carrying a lot of cargo!"

In back of Bill's truck, sat the remaining players from the Green River Rats. They included outfielders Niles Horton, Reggie Robertson, Silky Sullivan and Manny Polanco; and infielders Tubs McGraw, Danny Stanton and Cory Williamson.

"I know one thing," Frank said, as he watched his last two trucks continue down Main Street. "Those kids from Green River look like a confident bunch."

Frank couldn't quite put a finger on it as he watched the Rats' players wave to the crowd up ahead. It was an attitude all the Green River kids seemed to have, as if they were saying, "come on over to the park and watch the Rats devour the Tigers."

The parade continued down Main Street. Float after float

passed by. The Elks Club's Dixieland band passed by as did the 100-piece band from Grand Valley High School.

The Old-Timers Car Club of Johnsonville passed the bandstand with six Model-T automobiles, each one of them polished to the hilt and each one of them containing couples who were dressed in 1920s attire. The women were wearing colorful hats, and the men, ironically, were sporting Johnsonville Tigers' hats.

The final entrant, of course, was none other than Johnny Hayes himself, bringing up the rear was his bright red fire engine.

On the back end of the fire engine were two streamers. One said "God Bless America", the other said "Go Tigers."

It was now six o'clock in the evening and the baseball fans were already filling up the bleachers at Johnson Park.

The additional bleachers, up and down the third base lines which were constructed earlier in the year, would come in handy, but it still wouldn't be enough.

Some of the fans brought their own chairs and blankets and found a viewing area behind the left field fence and in front of the tall oak trees.

Johnny Treehorn, the assistant manager at the local supermarket, had just left in a van, after dropping off another load of hot dogs, hamburgers and plenty of buns. "I hope this will get us through," Mildred Robertson said to her co-workers—four teenage girls, who were already looking out the window of the snack bar, wondering how they were going to accommodate all the people.

Gabriel Martinez, the head maintence man at Johnsonville High, was busy putting the finishing touches on the infield, chalking up perfect lines, all the way up and down the first and third base lines. He finished up by rolling out perfect ovals to act as on-deck circles for both the visiting team and the home team.

Normally, Gabriel would stick to taking care of the baseball field at Johnson High, but he knew his friend, Carl Perkins, would have his hands full today.

And besides, Gabriel loved baseball, too. His family was already camped out in a nice spot, out beyond the center field fence. They had a big blanket, plenty of fried chicken and soft drinks to keep them happy for the entire game.

Both teams had stopped off at the high school and had completed an hour of batting practice, followed by 20 minutes of infield practice. The players were just now gathering in the outfield—the Tigers were out in right field, the Rats in left.

Filo Hamilton was giving his final pep talk to the Green River Rats. His assistant coach, Flavio Hamilton, Filo's father, stood next to him. Flavio was a big man—he stood 6-foot-4 and looked to weigh in the neighborhood of 300 pounds.

The Rats stood up and started to do some stretching. Billy, who was listening to last-minute instructions from Coach Perkins, took a glance toward left field. He saw Flavio talking to another big man...no it wasn't a man, it was Boomer McPherson.

"My goodness," said Lenny, who was also eyeballing the Rats. "Those guys are twice our size and look at that number 11. Billy, is that Boomer? Is that the kid nobody can get a hit off of?"

"That's him," Billy said, as he looked up at his coach.

"Now, listen guys," Carl said. "They put their pants on just like you do. They like baseball. They like to go to movies, roller skate, ride bikes and go on picnics just like you do. They're kids. Just like you.

"Let's stay focused. They are undefeated. We are undefeated. We have one more game to win. Now let's go out and do it."

The Tigers headed for their dugout on the first base side of the diamond; the Rats entered their dugout on the third base side.

The four umpires gathered at home plate, and were joined moments later by the two head coaches, Carl Perkins and Filo Hamilton.

The head umpire, Ross Burkhart, went over the ground rules and then tossed the coin to see which team would get the last at-bats. Carl called "heads" as the coin landed squarely on home plate. "Heads it is," Burkhart said. "Mr. Perkins, have your team take the field."

It was time to play ball. Behind home plate sat George, Claire and Joan. Right next to them sat the Turners and the O'Haras.

In the bleachers, behind the first base dugout, were Ezra Lockhart, his wife, Agnes, his daughter-in-law, Joanne, and his son, Leonard. Next to the Lockhart's were the Chow family, the Ramirez family and the Jameson family.

Out in left field Clancy Burnside was joined by his wife, Betty, who had just finished her shift at the supermarket. She sat down on the blanket, curled up in her husband's arms, gave him a big smile, and said, "Honey, this is the game we've been waiting for."

The Calhouns, who were forced to rush back to their ranch to take care of an injured calf, were late arrivals, but did manage to find a spot right next to the Burnsides. Matthew shook hands with Clancy. "Let's play ball," he said.

The announcer, Jimmy Smith, who had recently graduated from Johnsonville High and was to enroll at Colorado State in the fall, majoring in radio broadcasting, introduced the teams. The Wilkinson sisters, Rita Mae, Sandra and Barbara, who had recently won a high school talent contest over at Grand Valley, sang the Star Spangled Banner.

The umpires took their positions. The home plate umpire brushed off the plate. He fastened his chest protector and yelled, "Play ball!"

Chapter 10

The Championship Game

Carl Perkins had thought long and hard about starting Lenny. He had tried once before to keep an opponent off-balance by throwing all his pitchers in one game. He wasn't sure if anything was going to work against the Rats, but this would be his strategy. Carl looked over at his assistant coaches, Johnny and Cyrus, "Here we go," he said, as he turned his attention back to the mound and watched Lenny finish his warm-up pitches.

He looked over his infield. He had Jimmy at first, Clayton at second, Chucky at third and his ace in the hole, Billy at short.

Timmy was back in left field, Ryan in center and Michael in right. Carl watched his catcher, Corky, haul in Lenny's last warm-up pitch and fire the ball down to second.

Billy took the throw and flipped it to Clayton. Clayton fired the ball to Chucky, who tossed the game ball to Jimmy, who in turn handed the ball to his pitcher. Jimmy smiled at Lenny and said, "Let's do it."

Lenny took a deep breath, toed the rubber and unleashed the first pitch of the game. The Rats' second baseman and lead-off hitter, Silky Sullivan, swung and hit a come-backer right back at Lenny.

The ball banged off Lenny's glove and trickled out toward Billy at short. Billy grabbed the ball with his throwing hand and made a quick throw to first to nip Silky for the first out of the game.

The Johnsonville fans cheered. George stood up and yelled, "Way to go Billy!" George saw a camera flash just to the right of him. It was the photographer from the Grand Valley Dispatch, and standing next to him was Willard Smith.

George and Willard exchanged glances. George took off his Tigers' hat and tipped it toward Willard as if to say "What do you think of that?"

Bugs McPherson stepped to the plate. The first pitch from Lenny was high and outside. But on the very next pitch, Bugs bounced a high-hopper over the head of Chucky at third. Bugs was off and running and coasted into second with a double.

Billy took the throw-in from Timmy and took a quick look at Bugs. Bugs was smiling, but his lips were sealed. No sign of any creatures hovering around his cheeks.

Billy tossed the ball to Lenny and went back to his position at short. Lenny got his sign from Corky and threw a change-up to the next batter, Bumper McPherson. Bumper took a mighty cut and drilled a shot up the middle. Billy was quick to react. He moved to his left, dove and caught the ball on the fly.

Bugs was halfway to third when he stopped, turned and watched Billy flick the ball to Clayton for the double play.

Bugs threw his helmet down, put his hands on his hips and walked back to the Green River dugout. Filo Hamilton handed Bugs his catching gear and said, "Bugsy, get your head up, this game is just getting started."

Billy and Clayton were the last two players to reach the Tigers' dugout. High-fives were in order.

"Way to go out there," Carl Perkins said. "Great defense. Now let's see what we can do off this monster."

Billy grabbed his helmet, searched around for his Louisville Slugger and headed for the on-deck circle.

He kneeled and admired what he saw. Boomer didn't need a pitching mound, he was already tall enough. Billy watched him release his warm-up pitches. The pitches were crisp, and hard, and they bolted into Bugs' mitt, unleashing a sound that could be heard all over the park.

"Look at the size of that kid," Matthew Calhoun said. "He's throwing bullets out there. How are we going to get to this guy?"

"They say he's unhittable...fifteen strike outs in his last game," Clancy said. "Two perfect games to his credit. I wouldn't want to face him!"

Billy stepped to the plate. He had seen Boomer many, many times over the last few months in his dreams. But this time it was for real.

Billy planted his right foot. Elbow up. Eyes focused

squarely on the pitcher, just like his dad had told him a thousand times.

Boomer's first pitch sailed over Billy's head. Billy hit the dirt...his helmet flew off and bounced in front of the plate. The ball banged into the webbing of the backstop behind home plate. The ball just hung there...stuck in the webbing.

The crowd stood in awe. All eyes were on the ball. "My goodness", Claire said. "George did you see that pitch?"

"I don't think anybody saw that pitch!"

Billy returned to the batter's box. He waited for Boomer's next offering. He eyed Boomer's release point. The ball was on him in a flash and creased the corner of the plate.

"Strike one," yelled the umpire.

Billy stepped out of the box and took a deep breath. He checked to see if he had the trademark on the bat facing the right way. He placed the fingers of his left hand over his dad's branded signature. He held up his right hand, signaling to the home plate umpire for extra time.

Billy stepped back in the box and stared down Boomer. There was no reason to look for anything but a fastball.

Billy picked up the ball the moment it left Boomer's fingertips. Billy started his swing. He connected. The ball sizzled past Boomer, bounced over second base, and headed out toward center field.

Billy rounded first and came to a screeching halt as he watched Manny Polanco, the Green River centerfielder, scoop up the ball and make a perfect throw to second base.

"That's my grandson," George said, as he stood up and shook hands with anyone that was near him.

Billy had just recorded the first hit ever off Boomer

McPherson. Boomer was stunned. Filo called timeout and quickly jogged out to the pitcher's mound.

"How did he do that coach?" Boomer said.

"Boomer, it was just a hit...he got lucky. Settle down and mow these kids down."

"Okay, coach." Boomer didn't believe what just happened. But he wasn't about to let it happen again.

He got his sign from Bugs and rifled a fastball right down the middle to Clayton.

"Strike one...strike two...strike three."

The home plate umpire's right arm moved up and down like a pin-ball. Boomer fanned Clayton, Ryan O'Hara and Timmy Chow in succession. Billy was left stranded at first and after one inning of play, the crowd, and the players, took a breather.

The game was on.

Lenny looked like he was pitching uphill when he picked up the sign from Corky as the second inning got underway. Boomer was in the batter's box. His strike zone was as big as a telephone booth.

Lenny figured he wouldn't have any trouble throwing a strike to Boomer—the strike zone was certainly big enough, the question was how do you get a pitch past him.

Lenny couldn't.

Boomer smacked the first pitch into the Rats' dugout. The players scattered, as the ball careened off the dugout wall and bounced back into the playing field.

Boomer fouled Lenny's next pitch into the Tigers' dugout. Once again, the players scattered as the ball rattled around the floor of the dugout before coming to a screeching halt next to the water cooler.

"Try to jam him inside," Carl yelled from the steps of the dugout. "Don't let him extend his arms."

Easy for you to say, thought Lenny.

Lenny took another deep breath and tried to do what his coach had asked.

The pitch was inside, but Boomer had no trouble getting around on it. The ball took off like a rocket toward the left side of the infield. Unfortunately for Boomer and the Rats, Billy had timed it perfectly. Billy leaped and snared the ball right out of the air for the first out of the second inning.

Boomer trotted back to the dugout. He threw his hands in the air. "Who is that guy?"

Booker T was next and he sent a ball to deep right field, but Michael O'Hara was off at the crack of the bat and made the catch at the warning-track for the second out.

That left Ronnie Hamilton, the Rats' third-sacker, to get something started for Green River. He did get a pitch to his liking, but he too, flew out. This time, it was Ryan O'Hara, hauling in the fly ball, and surprisingly, the Tigers had kept the Rats off the scoreboard for two innings.

Boomer was relentless in the bottom of the inning. He fanned Chucky, Jimmy and Corky Calhoun. It took just ten pitches. Only one pitch got away from Boomer and it tore a hole in the backstop, bounced through an opening in the bleachers, and hopped though the window of the snack bar.

Mildred Robertson was just about to hand out a couple of sodas when the ball upended the cups. The first three children in line took the brunt of it. They headed for the bathroom in hopes of taking care of a sticky situation.

By the time the third inning rolled around, the fans were buzzing—especially the Johnsonville fans, who were amazed at how the Tigers had held off the much bigger Green River Rats.

But in the opening half of the third inning, things quickly changed as Rats' shortstop Tubs McGraw drilled a shot over the bag at third and scampered into second with an easy double.

Lenny walked the next batter, left-fielder Reggie Robertson, on four straight pitches. Carl quickly motioned to Johnny Hays to have Carlos warm up.

Billy and Clayton joined their coach on the mound and listened attentively as Carl talked to his starting pitcher. "Lenny, you have done just what I've asked you to do. But it's time to bring in Carlos. Let's see if we can continue to keep them off balance."

Carl patted Lenny on the back and handed the ball to Carlos. The Tigers' reliever finished his tosses and then prepared to do battle with the Rats' ninth batter in the lineup, Manny Polanco.

Manny had been told by his coach to "wait him out", but Carlos threw back-to-back strikes to put the Rats' batter in the hole, 0-2. Manny was forced to swing on the next pitch. He lunged for the ball and hit a one-hopper to the hole between third and short. Billy back-handed the ball, threw to Clayton for the first out, and the relay by the second-sacker was right on the money to Jimmy for the double play.

George, Claire and Joan stood up and clapped. "What a play," George said. "But we still need one more out."

With the go-ahead run at third in the person of Tugs Mc-Graw, Carlos went to work on the Rats' leadoff hitter, Silky Sullivan.

Silky smashed the first pitch from Carlos toward Billy at short. The ball took a bad hop, but Billy let the ball bounce off his chest. He scooped up the ball and threw a dart to Jimmy for the third out of the inning.

Billy ran off the field. The crowd began to chant: "Billy...Billy...Billy!" The Tigers shortstop was starting to make believers out of them all.

In the bottom of the third, Boomer was visibly upset. Things were not going as he had planned. "We should have put these guys away by now," he yelled at Bumper, as the Rats' first-sacker handed him the ball and returned to his position.

Boomer bore down. He struck out Michael O'Hara on five pitches. He fanned Lenny on three straight pitches. With two outs, Billy stepped in.

A breeze rolled in from the outfield as Boomer toed the rubber. The first pitch was just outside. The second just inside. The third was in the dirt. The fourth offering was just off the outside corner. "Ball four," yelled the umpire.

Boomer threw down the rosin bag in disgust. First he allowed him a hit, now he walks him. The breeze stopped. "What was that breeze all about?" he said out loud.

He made Clayton pay for the walk to Billy. Clayton got caught looking on three straight pitches. The Tigers and the Rats would move on to the fourth inning, deadlocked.

Carl made his next move. He sent Willie, the Tigers' hardest thrower, to the mound to start the fourth. The Rats were getting a little rattled and Carl hoped Willie's fastball would keep them honest.

Willie had his work cut out for him. He was now facing the "Rat Pack." Bugs, who had doubled in the first inning, did it again in the fourth, as he slammed an 0-2 pitch from Willie, down the right field line and into the corner for another double.

Bumper was next to bat and he hit a slow-roller back to the mound. Willie had no shot at Bugs, so he wheeled and threw to first to nip the slow-running Bumper by a step-and-a-half.

With Bugs on third and one out, Carl had Willie keep the ball away from Boomer. The Rats' big man trotted to first after walking on four straight pitches.

Now, with runners at the corners, Carl was hoping the Tigers could get out of the inning. But Booker T would have none of that as he singled up the middle, allowing Bugs to practically walk home with the first run of the game.

The Tigers were in trouble. With runners at the corners again, Willie fired a fastball on the outside corner to Ronnie Hamilton. Ronnie swung and sent a two-hopper to Clayton at second.

Clayton made his pivot, threw to Billy, who touched second and relayed his throw to first in time to nip Ronnie for another Tigers' double play.

But the damage was done. The Rats had the lead 1-0. The Tigers had just nine outs left.

Boomer just wouldn't let up as he sat down the Tigers

in order in the fourth and again in the fifth. But fortunately, so did Willie, as he made his parents—Milton and Elsie—proud as he shutdown the Rats as well.

In the top of sixth, Willie had Boomer to contend with to start the inning. Boomer hit Willie's first pitch high and deep to left field. Timmy ran all the way to the fence, turned, looked up, picked the ball up quickly, and made the catch.

The Chow family stood up and cheered. The Burnsides and the Calhouns, who all had ringside seats on the play, yelled in unison, "Way to go Timmy!"

The Rats continued to put the pressure on. Booker T and Ronnie Hamilton followed with back-to-back singles and once again the Tigers were in trouble.

Willie needed to get Tubs McGraw. He tried to keep the ball on the outside corner. The first two pitches were high and outside, but Willie came back to nip the corner on his next two offerings to even out the count.

The next throw was in the dirt to run the count full. Willie was forced to serve up the next pitch and Tubs was waiting.

He drilled a sizzling liner right at Billy. Billy with his quick release caught the ball and in one fluid motion unleashed his throw to first. Jimmy applied the tag to double up Ronnie, who had tried in vain to dive back to the bag safely.

The first base umpire was right on top of the play. He raised his right arm and yelled, "You're out!"

The Tigers had survived the top of the sixth without yielding a run, thanks to another double play from Billy.

The Johnsonville Tigers were coming to bat in the bottom

of the sixth—needing a run to tie and two runs to win the district championship.

Boomer McPherson completed his warm-up pitches. He needed just three more outs and the Rats would be district champions. He was confident. After all, he'd allowed just one hit and a walk to that pesky lead-off batter. He'd pitched a one hitter so far, struck out fifteen batters, and to top it off the Rats had the lead, 1-0.

No problem. He would just rare back and throw. They were home free. The championship was in the bag.

The Tigers were at the bottom of their order, the pitcher's spot. So it would be up to Willie Turner to get it going.

Willie settled into the batter's box and Billy moved into the on-deck circle. The breeze returned and Billy glanced out toward left field. The branches of the tall oak trees beyond the fence were swirling. A few low white clouds barely visible were moving in over the field and the lights flickered for a moment...and then came on...as darkness was settling in.

"Come on Willie, you got to get on," yelled Milton. Elsie crossed her fingers. The Johnsonville fans all began to clap in unison.

The wind picked up. A dust-devil swirled like a miniature tornado as it made its way across the infield.

Boomer got his sign from Bugs and sent a blazing fastball toward the plate. "Ball one," roared the umpire as the ball just missed the outside corner of the plate.

Bugs threw the ball back to his brother. Boomer cuffed the ball in his big hands and rubbed his fingers across its red-threaded seams. He looked up at the sky. "What's with this wind?"

Boomer's next pitch was high and inside as Willie barely had time to get out of the batter's box. "Ball two," yelled the umpire.

The wind picked up even more. The fans were forced to hold on to their hats. A hot dog wrapper came to a stop right on home plate. The umpire called time and picked up the wrapper and at the same time took the brush from his back pocket and cleaned the plate.

The umpire returned to his position and signaled to Willie to return to the batter's box. Boomer's next pitch was again offline...this time the ball sailed over the umpire's head. "Ball three."

The wind continued. Boomer fired the next pitch. The ball was low as it ripped through the dirt in front of the plate and bounced off Bugs' chest protector.

"Ball four!"

Willie was on. The Johnsonville fans roared.

Boomer returned to the pitching rubber. Filo Hamilton called time out and rushed out to the mound. Bugs took off his catcher's mask and trotted out to join the meeting.

"Come on Boomer," yelled Filo. "We need just three outs. You've done it a hundred times. Strike these guys out and let's go home!"

"But coach, this wind, it's driving me nuts."

"What wind?"

The three of them looked up in the air. The clouds were gone. The wind was gone. The sky had turned black and they could see hundreds of stars above—each one of them glowing, pulsating, as if each had a heart and their own special heartbeat.

The players returned to their positions. Billy left the on-deck circle and walked slowly to the plate. The fans were on their feet. "Billy...Billy...Billy!"

Billy took his stance. Boomer released the pitch. The ball rocketed into Bugs' mitt. The impact knocked Bugs down, but he managed to hang onto the ball. He looked up in time to watch the umpire raise his right hand.

"Strike one!"

Bugs returned the ball to Boomer. "Now we got you," the Green River catcher said, as he smiled at Billy and returned to his spot behind the plate.

Boomer toed the rubber. He had just thrown his best pitch of the night and he was about to give the pesky kid at the plate another.

Billy stepped back in. He touched the barrel of the bat one more time. He remembered what his dad had always said. "Watch the release, son. Pick the ball up early and good things will happen."

The fans started to chant once again. George, Claire and Joan were on their feet.

Boomer gripped the baseball. He toed the rubber. He heard his brother yell from behind the plate. "Let her rip."

Boomer fired. It was the hardest pitch he had ever thrown in his life. The ball zipped toward the plate.

Billy could see the seams of the ball as it left Boomer's hand. Billy swung.

Crack!

Billy connected. He got it all. The ball sailed over the head of the Green River shortstop Tubs McGraw. The ball continued to rise into the dark sky.

Bugs dropped his catcher's mask, stood on home plate and watched the flight of the ball. Boomer turned to look, but there was no need to—the sound alone had already signaled his fate.

Clancy Burnside stood up. "This ball has a chance!"

"It's out-a-here," yelled Matthew Calhoun, as he looked straight up, just in time to pick up the flight of the orbiting oval.

The Rats' left fielder, Reggie Robertson, raced back to the edge of the fence. He looked up and watched the ball sail over the fence and disappear into the oak trees.

Billy took off for first base. The crowd looked up as the fireworks from Nob Hill began to light up the horizon. Willie touched home plate as the booming sounds of the fireworks roared through the park.

Billy scampered around third with both hands high in the air. He crossed home plate and was greeted by the rest of the Tigers.

The players raised him up onto their shoulders as the Johnsonville fans stood up and cheered.

The Johnsonville Tigers had won the District Title and Billy had his *Victory*, in more ways than one.

Epilogue

Joan Reynolds frantically searched for the keys to Belle. She was sure her father kept them in the desk in the back room of the Clown's Den. She finally tried the bottom drawer. There they were. She glanced at her watch. She had twenty minutes to get out to Golden Hills, pick up her parents, and get over to Roscoe's—everybody was waiting.

It was her parent's 50th wedding anniversary, and to top it off it was Saturday, and the New York Yankees were playing the Boston Red Sox on national television.

Joan started up Belle, backed the old jeep out of the carport, pulled out of the driveway and headed for Golden Hills.

It would take her about ten minutes to get to her parent's retirement home. George and Claire had moved into the place, just weeks ago. Joan shook her head as she sped down the highway. Her father had fought the change, but now that he was settled in, he was getting used to the old folks' life style, as he would put it.

Joan had rented out her house over on Fourth Street and

moved into her parent's place. She had plans to turn the home into a bed-and-breakfast business. Johnsonville had grown by leaps and bounds over the last ten years. The population had doubled, investors had moved in, new homes were going up everywhere. Johnsonville had turned into a resort town.

George and Claire were waiting as Joan pulled Belle into the driveway.

"Why did you bring Belle?" George said, as he helped Claire edge her way into the back seat.

"It's your anniversary," Joan said. "I didn't want to leave her out of this. This is a big day. I thought it would be only fitting to include Belle."

"I guess you're right," Claire said. "I'm getting a little old to get in and out of this jeep, but I guess we'd better hurry, I know everybody's waiting. It's going to be standing room only down there."

It was the summer of 1972. Ten years had passed since Billy Ray had turned Johnsonville upside down with that homerun of his, And now, Roscoe's Sports Pub would be jam-packed with Johnsonville baseball fans, all of them hoping to get a chance to see Billy Ray Reynolds play again— only this time they would get to see him take the field at Yankee Stadium.

Frank O'Hara had gone into business with George and Claire in 1970. They purchased the red brick building at the corner of First Street and Main and made it into Johnsonville's first sports pub.

It was only fitting that it would be called Roscoe's. George certainly had no problem coming up with enough pictures and trophies to decorate every wall in the place.

Joan turned left on to Main Street. Claire glanced over at the new furniture store that now covered an entire block on the north side of the street. "I just can't get used to it," Claire said. "Everytime I pass by here...our drugstore is gone...the old café is gone. It just seems like yesterday, Billy and Chipper were running in through the front door—rattling those chimes."

"Well, get used to it, honey." George said. "Besides we made a little money on that deal. Downtown just doesn't look the same anymore. But, it's a good thing. Johnsonville's growing, times change. We need to change with it."

Joan pulled Belle into the new parking lot adjacent to Roscoe's. She led her parents in through the front door of the Pub. They were greeted to a lot of cheers and whistling.

"Happy anniversary, you two," Carl Perkins said, as he was first to greet the couple.

Johnny Hayes and Cyrus Jones pulled two chairs out from under the long table that was set up especially for the party-goers.

"I've never seen so many old people in one place," George said jokingly, as he and Claire took their seats.

Two-thousand miles away, Billy Ray Reynolds sat in the Yankee's locker room. He put away the telegram he had just received from his mother and put it in the back pocket of his Yankee's pinstriped uniform.

The telegram was signed "good luck" from all the gang at Roscoe's. He would keep it in his pocket until the final out of today's game; it would remind him of how many people had helped him get here—to Yankee Stadium, to fulfill his dream of playing in the major leagues.

It had once been his dad's dream. Then, his. And now, he was just an hour away from taking the field as a member of the New York Yankees.

Billy grabbed his bat, walked down the corridor and into the bright sunlight. He looked up into the clear blue sky, tipped his Yankee hat and said:

"We're here, Pop."

Billy felt a slight breeze. He looked out toward the infield and caught a glimpse of a swirling dust devil pick up steam, roll on out to centerfield and then disappear high above the confines of Yankee Stadium.

The Johnsonville Tigers

Clayton Burnside
Corky Calhoun
Timmy Chow
Chucky Jameson
Jimmy Jameson
Lenny Lockhart
Michael O'Hara
Ryan O'Hara
Carlos Ramirez
Billy Ray Reynolds
Willie Turner

The Green River Rats

Booker T McPherson

Boomer McPherson

Bugs McPherson

Bumper McPherson

Ronnie Hamilton

Woodrow Harrington

Niles Horton

Tubs McGraw

Manny Polanco

Reggie Robertson

Danny Stanton

Silky Sullivan

Cory Williamson

The Johnsonville Tigers' winning season

Tigers 3 Clarkson 1

Tigers 9 Carbon City 0

Tigers 4 Ridgedale 2

Tigers 5 Brighton 0

Tigers 7 Red Oak 4

Tigers 2 Clarkson 1

Tigers 8 Carbon City 0

Tigers 5 Ridgedale 2

Tigers 6 Brighton 1

Tigers 2 Red Oak 0

District Championship

Tigers 2 Green River 1

The Championship Game

Johnsonville Tigers 2   Green River Rats 1

1	2	3	4	5	6	R	H	E
0	0	0	1	0	0	1	6	0
0	0	0	0	0	2	2	2	0

WP Willie Turner   LP Boomer McPherson

2B Bugs McPherson (2), Tubs McGraw; HR Billy Ray Reynolds